MW00535034

Electricity and Magnetism

Connecting Students to Science Series

By
JOHN B. BEAVER, Ph.D. and DON POWERS, Ph.D.

COPYRIGHT © 2003 Mark Twain Media, Inc.

ISBN 1-58037-222-8

Printing No. CD-1568

Mark Twain Media, Inc., Publishers
Distributed by Carson-Dellosa Publishing Company, Inc.

HPSO 216489

Table of Contents

Introduction to the Series

The Connecting Students to Science Series is designed for grades 5–8. The series introduces the following topics: Simple Machines, Electricity and Magnetism, Rocks and Minerals, Atmosphere and Weather, Chemistry, Light and Color, Sound, and The Solar System. Each book contains an introduction to the topic, naive concepts, inquiry activities, content integration, children's literature connections, curriculum resources, assessment documents, materials lists, and a bibliography.

Students will develop an understanding of the concepts and processes of science through the use of good scientific techniques. Students will be engaged in higher-level thinking skills while participating in fun and interesting activities. All of the activities are aligned with the National Science Education Standards and National Council of Teachers of Mathematics Standards.

This series is written for classroom teachers, parents, families, and students. The books in this series can be used as a full unit of study or as individual lessons to supplement existing textbooks or curriculum programs. Activities are designed to be pedagogically sound, hands-on, minds-on science activities that support the National Science Education Standards (NSES). Parents and students could use this series as an enhancement to what is being done in the classroom or as a tutorial at home.

The procedures and content background are clearly explained in the introduction and within the individual activities. Materials used in the activities are commonly found in classrooms and homes. If teachers are giving letter grades for the activities, points may be awarded for each level of mastery indicated on the assessment rubrics. If not, simple check marks at the appropriate levels will give students feedback on how well they are doing.

Introduction to the Concepts: Historical Perspective

Static Electricity

An awareness of static or electrostatic charge dates back to the Greek scientist Thales of Miletus, 600 B.C. We are all familiar with the effects of walking across a carpet and touching a doorknob or having a thin plastic bag stick to our clothing. These and other examples are representative of electric fields that are stationary or static, as opposed to a flowing charge or current electricity.

Benjamin Franklin observed static charges resulting from rubbing a hard rubber rod with rabbit fur and a glass rod with silk. He called the charges that were produced **negative** and **positive**, respectively. The practice of referring to a material that has gained electrons as having a negative charge and a material that has lost electrons as having a positive charge is still in use today.

William Gilbert (1540–1603) observed that rubbing a piece of amber allowed it to attract lightweight materials. He is credited with giving the name *electricity* to this property of matter. The word electricity is derived from the Greek word for amber, *elektron*.

Dr. Galvani (1737–98) of Bologna, Italy, worked with electrostatic devices in his laboratory and noted the influence that static electricity had on a frog's leg. The leg twitched when a scalpel he was using apparently conducted a charge from one of his machines to a nerve in the frog's leg. This observation led to the eventual discovery of the electric battery.

Allesandro Volta (1745–1827) invented the **battery** in 1800 by layering silver and zinc plates separated by leather strips soaked in salt. This "pile" developed a fairly significant charge when the bottom silver and top zinc strips in the pile were connected or touched simultaneously. Early uses for the voltaic pile included using it to separate water into its two elements. Wires were connected to the pile and attached to metal pieces called **electrodes** that were placed in the water. A small amount of acid was added to the water to improve its conductivity. The process of using electricity to induce a chemical change was known as **electrolysis**. The use of electrolysis led to the discovery of several new elements.

Current Electricity

In our discussion of **static electricity**, it becomes clear that it is defined as the charge-producing movement of electrons within a material and between materials. When electrons flow freely over a substance, we have what is called **electric current**. Some materials, such as most metals, conduct this flow of electrons more readily than other materials.

Wires correctly connecting a flashlight battery and a light bulb make a complete circuit. The glow of the light bulb leads to the inference that electrons are flowing. The electrons are present in the wires, and the flashlight battery serves as the motive force to set them in motion. If you had a row of ball bearings in a plastic tube and rolled an additional ball bearing into the tube, energy would be transferred from ball to ball along the length of the tube. This is analogous to how electrons flow through a wire. The electrons flow from one electrode in a battery, through the circuit, and into the other electrode on the battery. The flow of electrons is from the electrode on the battery labeled with the negative "-" sign and to the electrode labeled with the positive "+" sign.

2

Introduction to the Concepts: Historical Perspective (cont.)

Georg Ohm (1787–1854) developed the understanding of how voltage, resistance, and current are related and stated this relationship in Ohm's Law. Ohm started his career as an elementary school teacher, and later taught in secondary school. During his free time, he studied the factors that affected the flow of electricity across various metal conductors. **Ohm's Law** may be simply represented in the following mathematical equation: $E = IR$, where E stands for electromotive force or volts, I for electric current or amperes, and R stands for resistance or ohms. There is always some resistance to the flow of electricity, and Ohm's law provides a means for expressing the resistance, relative to voltage and amperage. The measurement of voltage is used to find the resistance in a system. A voltmeter is placed at any place in a circuit to find the drop in voltage.

Magnetism

Thales (600 B.C.), a Greek scientist, noted the attractive force in a natural earth material called **lodestone** (leading stone), which was made up of iron ore. Observations of lodestone included noting that a slender piece of the mineral, when suspended from a string, oriented itself with the North and South Poles of the earth.

William Gilberte (1540–1603) published the first book dealing with magnetism in 1600. He noted that the earth acts as a giant magnet, and opposite poles attract each other.

A magnetic field represents an area around a magnet that may influence other materials. For instance, a magnetized iron bar will attract or repel other objects made of a similar material. A magnetic field may be observed by placing a magnet under a piece of paper and scattering iron filings over it. It may be observed in a bar magnet that the two magnetic fields exist, one at either end of the bar magnet. These areas are called **magnetic poles**. A bar magnet suspended from a string will align itself with the Poles of the earth. It may also be observed that when two magnets are brought together, like poles repel each other, and unlike poles attract each other.

Hans Christian Oersted (1777–1851) discovered the magnetic field that exists around electrical circuits. A magnetic compass placed near a wire with an electric current flowing through it will be deflected in a regular pattern. Additionally, a wire placed vertically through a horizontal piece of cardboard (Figure 1) will exhibit a magnetic field when iron filings are sprinkled onto the cardboard.

Figure 1

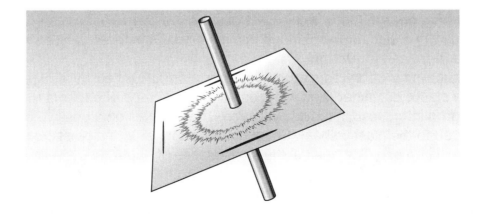

Introduction to the Concepts: Historical Perspective (cont.)

Since a magnetic field can be detected around an active circuit, a compass may be used to detect an electric current. The instrument used for measuring small electric currents is called a **galvanometer**. The galvanometer uses a permanent magnet and a small coil of wire or spring suspended near the permanent magnet. When a small current is introduced near the coil, it behaves like a magnet. The interaction of the temporary magnet (spring) and the permanent magnet is used to produce a measure of electric field (Figure 2).

Michael Faraday (1791–1867) and Joseph Henry (1791–1878) discovered that a magnet moving in the vicinity of a coil of wire would generate an electric current. This is known as **induced current**. The large electric generators used today in power plants all over the world are based on the principles of induction outlined by Faraday and Henry.

Wrapping an insulated wire around a nail, and then attaching the ends of the wire to a battery, is a way to create a temporary magnet called an **electromagnet**. The use of magnets to induce electrical currents and the use of electric currents to produce magnetic fields are examples of the relationship between magnetic and electrical charges.

The galvanometer, as seen in the diagram below, is a device that can be used to detect and measure small amounts of current. The movable coil becomes a temporary magnet when current flows, deflecting a spring to the right or left. The amount of movement in the spring and attached needle is relative to the amount of current.

Figure 2

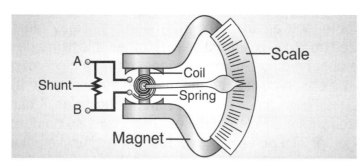

In Amir D. Aczel's book, *The Riddle of the Compass: The Invention That Changed the World*, he recounts the history of the magnetic compass, from its use by the Chinese to orient buildings, to its application by the Italians in navigation at sea.

Static Electricity Concepts

Static electricity or stationary charges are the result of the migration or transfer of electrons. A **positive charge** forms when electrons are removed from a material, and a **negative charge** forms when electrons are added to a material. Objects acquire a static charge by **friction**, **conduction**, and **induction**.

A charge may be introduced in a balloon that is rubbed by a piece of wool through **friction**. If a plastic container filled with confetti-sized scraps of paper is rubbed with a plastic bag, a charge is introduced in the lid by friction. The lid takes on a positive charge as electrons are transferred to the plastic sheet. Small pieces of paper in the plastic container can be observed standing on end. The ends of the small pieces of paper near the lid become negatively charged, and the ends of the pieces of paper away from the lid become positively charged. This is an example of an induced charge, as the electrons in the pieces of paper migrate to one end of the papers. The pieces of paper appear to stand on end and dance at the bottom of the

Introduction to the Concepts: Historical Perspective (cont.)

container, because the lid with a positive charge attracts the negative portion of the paper scraps. Note that when a material is given a charge through induction, the charge is opposite the object inducing the charge. Some of the pieces of paper may actually stick to the underside of the lid and lose their electrons to it. In this example, the charge is transferred through direct contact or **conduction**.

It can be observed that objects with like charges repel each other, while objects with opposite charges attract each other, and a charged object attracts a neutral object.

Other concepts that are related to static electric charges include the following. Static electric charges can be detected and measured, and static electric charges can be stored. A high level of **humidity** (water vapor in the air) will cause charges on an object to dissipate more rapidly than when the air is dry.

Current Electricity Concepts

The concept of a circuit is related to the root of the word *circuit* or *circle*, and just as a circle is represented by a closed figure, the **circuit** represents a continuous path through which electricity flows. Basic elements of a circuit include an energy source, a conductor or wire for transmitting the electricity, and usually an appliance or resistor. An example might include a simple circuit made up of a "D-Cell" flashlight battery, a piece of bell wire, and a small flashlight bulb (Figure 3). Such a circuit is called a **closed or complete circuit**.

Figure 3

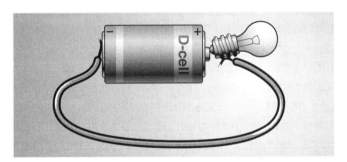

A **switch** may be added to open the circuit and turn off the light or to close the circuit and turn on the light. Switches are devices used to open and close circuits.

Short circuits occur when the current finds a path with lower resistance than the circuit that is intended. For instance, a short circuit will result if, instead of using a low-resistance wire to connect a light bulb in a circuit, the wire is used to connect the negative end and the positive end of a battery directly. In this situation, the wire will rapidly heat up, and the battery will be depleted in a short time.

Circuits can be configured in a number of different ways, and both the sources and devices that are used in a circuit can be connected in different ways. Circuits can be designed to perform a variety of useful functions.

A subtopic related to electricity is that of conductors and insulators. It is best to think of a continuum or relative scale with materials that are excellent conductors at one end of the scale and materials that are poor conductors at the other end of the scale. Materials that either do not conduct electricity or conduct it poorly are considered **insulators**.

Naive Concepts

Students and adults have many naive conceptions when it comes to electricity and magnetism. Much of this is apparently due to the fact that we are dealing with "black boxes," or invisible forces. One of the best sources for the naive ideas related to electricity and magnetism is the program *Operation Physics*. The following represents a presentation of some of the naive concepts that will be addressed in the activities included in this book. Note that the presentation of the naive concepts is followed by a presentation of the accepted science concepts. Additionally, the following website is an excellent source for naive concepts in science: www.ems.psu.edu/~fraser/BadScience.html.

Static Electricity

The idea that objects carry a negative or positive charge represents a source for several naive concepts. Students may accept the idea that substances carry opposite charges; however, this may lead to the intuitive idea that if materials that are negatively charged have an excess of electrons, then materials with a positive charge have an excess of protons. The scientific generalization is based on the ability of materials to freely give up or take on **electrons**; therefore, a positive charge forms when a substance has lost electrons, and a negative charge forms when a material takes on electrons.

Students may also think that materials that lose electrons have lost them completely. The view from science is that there is a conservation of charge and that a material may temporarily give up electrons to nearby materials, but there is no net loss of electrons. In time, a charged object will either regain lost electrons or give up extra electrons, and return to a neutral state.

Students may come to the conclusion that all atoms are charged, since they observe interaction among many different materials. They may also conclude that a charged object will only affect another charged object. The accepted view in science is that many materials carry no charge and are considered neutral, and a charged object attracts a neutral object. Furthermore, objects can acquire a charge through **friction**, **conduction**, and **induction**.

Circuits

Many of the naive concepts relative to current electricity and circuits are related to an incomplete understanding of a complete circuit. Students may accept that electricity flows from an energy source, such as a battery, through a wire to a light bulb. However, they may not realize that in order for the circuit to be complete, the electrons must continue in a path back to the source (battery). A **circuit** is a continuous path of flowing electrons from a source, through wires and appliances (resistors), and back to the source.

A common understanding is that conductors allow electricity to flow through them and that insulators do not allow current to flow. This concept is related to resistance, or the relative ability of a material to allow electrons to flow.

A more acceptable view involves looking at the nature of conductors. A material is a conductor when it has electrons that are free to move. There are a number of variables involved in whether a substance is a conductor or a nonconductor. Included in these variables is the nature of the material, its thickness, temperature, and other factors. Usually, **insulators** have

6

Naive Concepts (cont.)

relatively few electrons that are free to move, whereas **conductors** have many electrons that are free to move. Generally speaking, shorter wires are better conductors, thicker wires are better conductors, and some metals are better conductors than others. Gold is one of the best conductors, followed by silver; however, their cost is too high for wide use. Copper is frequently used, because it is a good conductor with other properties that make it popular for use as a conductor, including its cost and flexibility.

One of the most popular misconceptions about electricity is that batteries have electricity inside them, as opposed to the accepted scientific view that chemical energy can be converted to electricity. Other forms of energy can also be converted to electricity, including solar energy. Falling water, tides, and the wind are all used to produce electricity, and all have the sun as their original source of energy.

Properties and Behaviors of Magnets

Early explorations with magnets and magnetism may be related to several misunderstandings about the properties and behaviors of magnets. Children may conclude, incorrectly, that all metals or metal-colored objects are attracted to magnets. They may also conclude that all magnets are made of iron, since it is one of the more accessible materials for use in the elementary or middle-school classroom. They may also believe that larger magnets are stronger than smaller magnets. More widely held beliefs include the idea that the geographic and magnetic poles of the earth are in the same place, and that the magnetic poles of the earth are north in the northern hemisphere, and south in the southern hemisphere.

More extensive investigations with magnets and magnetism show us that magnets attract some metals, and materials that are attracted have magnetic properties. Magnets are made of various materials and come in a variety of shapes, sizes, and strengths. We also learn that the concentration of magnetism is in two places, or **poles**, on a magnet.

The earth acts as a giant magnet, and a freely suspended magnet in the northern hemisphere will orient itself with the North Pole. The pole of the magnet that points to the north is called a north pole, and the pole of the magnet that points to the south is called the south pole. This appears to be counter-intuitive, since we learn through exploration that opposite poles of a magnet attract, and like poles repel each other. This is a figment of history, and may be related to an early scientist simply labeling the end of the magnet that is oriented to the north with an "N," and the end pointing to the south pole with an "S."

Naive Concepts (cont.)

Magnetism Concepts

Exploration with magnets leads to the generalization that magnets attract some metals. We also find out that magnets have areas where their strength is maximized. We call these areas **poles**. Every magnet has two poles; one pole is referred to as the north pole, and the other is called the south pole. Additionally, we find that like poles repel each other, and unlike poles attract each other.

The earth acts as a giant magnet with a north pole and a south pole. The pole of a freely suspended magnet that points toward the earth's north is called a north pole. The pole that points to the earth's south is called a south pole. You will note that this is contrary to what we learn through exploration with magnets. It is an accepted convention in science to refer to the end of a freely swinging magnet pointing to the earth's north pole as the "north-seeking pole" or north pole of the magnet. Likewise, the south pole of a magnet is the end of the magnet that points in the direction of the earth's south pole.

Materials that are attracted to a magnet are magnetic materials. Magnets and magnetic materials contain "tiny magnets" called magnetic domains, and materials exhibit magnetic properties when these magnetic domains become aligned. Magnets come in a variety of sizes, shapes, and strengths. Heating, jarring, shaking, or dropping a magnet can destroy its magnetism.

Definitions of Terms

Static Electricity Terms
Static electricity is defined as electricity at rest.

Electrostatic charge is a charge that is confined to an object; that is, the object has taken on or lost electrons, and therefore has a net negative or positive charge.

Current Electricity Terms
Conductor is a material that allows an electric charge (electrons) to flow through it. Some conductors are better than others. Most metals are good conductors.

Insulator is a material that restricts an electric charge from flowing through it. Some insulators may be considered nonconductors.

Ampere is the measure for the unit of current.

Electric circuit is a closed-loop conducting path that consists of an energy source, an appliance or electric load, and wires that conduct the electric current from the battery, through the appliance, and back to the battery.

Electric current is the rate of flow of charge past a given point in an electric circuit.

Electricity is the physical attraction and repulsion of electrons within and between materials.

Definitions of Terms (cont.)

Electrification is the process of charging a body by adding or removing electrons.

Electromotive force (**emf**) is the energy per unit of charge supplied by a source of electricity.

Ohm is the measure for the unit of resistance in electric current.

Parallel circuit is a circuit with two or more appliances that are connected to provide separate conducting paths for current for each appliance.

Resistance is the opposition to flow of electricity.

Series circuit is a circuit with two or more appliances that are connected to provide a single conducting path for current.

Volt is the measure for the unit of potential difference.

Magnetism Terms

Domain is a microscopic magnetic region composed of a group of atoms whose magnetic fields are aligned in a common direction. A magnet has many magnetic domains that are all aligned in the same direction.

Line of flux (line of force) is a line around a pole of a magnet representing the direction of magnetic field.

Magnetic field is a region in which a magnetic force can be detected.

Magnetic flux is defined as lines of flux in a magnetic field, considered collectively. Magnetic flux can be observed by placing a magnet under a piece of paper, then scattering iron filings over the paper.

Magnetic force is a force associated with the motion of electric charges and can be measured indirectly by finding out how many similar objects a magnet can pick up.

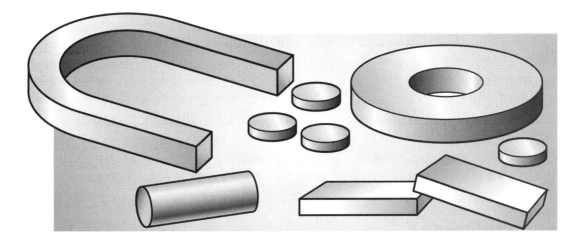

National Standards in Science, Math, and Technology

NSES Content Standards (NRC, 1996)

National Research Council (1996). *National Science Education Standards.* Washington, D.C.:
    National Academy Press.

UNIFYING CONCEPTS: K-12

Systems, Order, and Organization - The natural and designed world is complex. Scientists and students learn to define small portions for the convenience of investigation. The units of investigation can be referred to as systems. A system is an organized group of related objects or components that form a whole. Systems can consist of electrical circuits.

Systems, Order, and Organization

The goal of this standard is to ...

- Think and analyze in terms of systems.
- Assume that the behavior of the universe is not capricious. Nature is predictable.
- Understand the regularities in a system.
- Understand that prediction is the use of knowledge to identify and explain observations.
- Understand that the behavior of matter, objects, organisms, or events has order and can be described statistically.

Evidence, Models, and Explanation

The goal of this standard is to ...

- Recognize that evidence consists of observations and data on which to base scientific explanations.
- Recognize that models have explanatory power.
- Recognize that scientific explanations incorporate existing scientific knowledge (laws, principles, theories, paradigms, models), and new evidence from observations, experiments, or models.
- Recognize that scientific explanations should reflect a rich scientific knowledge base, evidence of logic, higher levels of analysis, greater tolerance of criticism and uncertainty, and a clear demonstration of the relationship between logic, evidence, and current knowledge.

Change, Constancy, and Measurement

The goal of this standard is to …

- Recognize that some properties of objects are characterized by constancy, including the speed of light, the charge of an electron, and the total mass plus energy of the universe.
- Recognize that changes might occur in the properties of materials, position of objects, motion, and form and function of systems.
- Recognize that changes in systems can be quantified.
- Recognize that measurement systems may be used to clarify observations.

National Standards in Science, Math, and Technology (cont.)

Form and Function

The goal of this standard is to …

- Recognize that the form of an object is frequently related to its use, operation, or function.
- Recognize that function frequently relies on form.
- Recognize that form and function apply to different levels of organization.
- Enable students to explain function by referring to form, and explain form by referring to function.

NSES Content Standard A: Inquiry

- Abilities necessary to do scientific inquiry
  - Identify questions that can be answered through scientific investigations.
  - Design and conduct a scientific investigation.
  - Use appropriate tools and techniques to gather, analyze, and interpret data.
  - Develop descriptions, explanations, predictions, and models using evidence.
  - Think critically and logically to make relationships between evidence and explanations.
  - Recognize and analyze alternative explanations and predictions.
  - Communicate scientific procedures and explanations.
  - Use mathematics in all aspects of scientific inquiry.
- Understanding about inquiry
  - Different kinds of questions suggest different kinds of scientific investigations.
  - Current scientific knowledge and understanding guide scientific investigations.
  - Mathematics is important in all aspects of scientific inquiry.
  - Technology used to gather data enhances accuracy and allows scientists to analyze and quantify results of investigations.
  - Scientific explanations emphasize evidence, have logically consistent arguments, and use scientific principles, models, and theories.
  - Science advances through legitimate skepticism.
  - Scientific investigations sometimes result in new ideas and phenomena for study, generate new methods or procedures, or develop new technologies to improve data collection.

NSES Content Standard B: Physical Science (Transfer of Energy) 5–8

- Energy is a property of many substances and is associated with heat, light, electricity, mechanical motion, sound, nuclei, and the nature of a chemical; energy is transferred in many ways.
- Electrical circuits provide a means of transferring electrical energy when heat, light, sound, or chemical changes are produced.
- In most chemical and nuclear reactions, energy is transferred into or out of a system. Heat, light, mechanical motion, or electricity might all be involved in such transfers.

National Standards (cont.)

NSES Content Standard D: Earth and Space Science 5–8
- Structure of the Earth System
  - The earth's magnetic field

NSES Content Standard E: Science and Technology 5–8
- Abilities of technological design
  - Identify appropriate problems for technological design.
  - Design a solution or product.
  - Implement the proposed design.
  - Evaluate completed technological designs or products.
  - Communicate the process of technological design.
- Understanding about science and technology
  - Scientific inquiry and technological design have similarities and differences.
  - Many people in different cultures have made, and continue to make, contributions.
  - Science and technology are reciprocal.
  - Perfectly designed solutions do not exist.
  - Technological designs have constraints.
  - Technological solutions have intended benefits and unintended consequences.

NSES Content Standard F: Science in Personal and Social Perspectives 5–8
- Science and Technology in Society
  - Science influences society through its knowledge and world view.
  - Societal challenges often inspire questions for scientific research.
  - Technology influences society through its products and processes.
  - Scientists and engineers work in many different settings.
  - Science cannot answer all questions, and technology cannot solve all human problems.

NSES Content Standard G: History and Nature of Science 5–8
- Science as a human endeavor
- Nature of science
  - Scientists formulate and test their explanations of nature using observation, experiments, and theoretical and mathematical models.
  - It is normal for scientists to differ with one another about interpretation of evidence and theory.
  - It is part of scientific inquiry for scientists to evaluate the results of other scientists' work.
- History of science
  - Many individuals have contributed to the traditions of science.
  - Science has been, and is, practiced by different individuals in different cultures.
  - Tracing the history of science can show how difficult it was for scientific innovators to break through the accepted ideas of their time to reach the conclusions we now accept.

National Standards (cont.)

Standards for Technological Literacy (STL) ITEA, 2000
International Technology Education Association (2000). *Standards for Technological Literacy.* Reston, VA: International Technology Education Association.

The Nature of Technology
Students will develop an understanding of the:
1. Characteristics and scope of technology.
2. Core concepts of technology.
3. Relationships among technologies and the connections between technology and other fields of study.

Technology and Society
Students will develop an understanding of the:
4. Cultural, social, economic, and political effects of technology.
5. Effects of technology on the environment.
6. Role of society in the development and use of technology.
7. Influence of technology on history.

Design
Students will develop an understanding of the:
8. Attributes of design.
9. Engineering design.
10. Role of trouble-shooting, research and development, invention and innovation, and experimentation in problem solving.

Abilities for a Technological World
Students will develop abilities to:
11. Apply the design process.
12. Use and maintain technological products and systems.
13. Assess the impact of products and systems.

The Designed World
Students will develop an understanding of and be able to select and use:
14. Medical technologies.
15. Agricultural and related biotechnologies.
16. Energy and power technologies.
17. Information and communication technologies.
18. Transportation technologies.
19. Manufacturing technologies.
20. Construction technologies.

National Standards (cont.)

Principles and Standards for School Mathematics (NCTM), 2000

National Council for Teachers of Mathematics (2000). *Principles and Standards for School Mathematics.* Reston, VA: National Council for Teachers of Mathematics.

Number and Operations
Students will be enabled to:
- Understand numbers, ways of representing numbers, relationships among numbers, and number systems.
- Understand meanings of operations and how they relate to one another.
- Compute fluently and make reasonable estimates.

Algebra
Students will be enabled to:
- Understand patterns, relations, and functions.
- Represent and analyze mathematical situations and structures using algebraic symbols.
- Use mathematical models to represent and understand quantitative relationships.
- Analyze change in various contexts.

Geometry
Students will be enabled to:
- Analyze characteristics and properties of two- and three-dimensional geometric shapes and develop mathematical arguments about geometric relationships.
- Specify locations and describe spatial relationships using coordinate geometry and other representational systems.
- Apply transformations and use symmetry to analyze mathematical situations.
- Use visualization, spatial reasoning, and geometric modeling to solve problems.

Measurement
Students will be enabled to:
- Understand measurable attributes of objects and the units, systems, and processes of measurement.
- Apply appropriate techniques, tools, and formulas to determine measurements.

Data Analysis and Probability
Students will be enabled to:
- Formulate questions that can be addressed with data and collect, organize, and display relevant data to answer them.
- Select and use appropriate statistical methods to analyze data.
- Develop and evaluate inferences and predictions that are based on data.
- Understand and apply basic concepts of probability.

Science Process Skills

Introduction: Science is organized curiosity, and an important part of this organization includes the thinking skills or information-processing skills. We ask the question "why?" and then must plan a strategy for answering the question or questions. In the process of answering our questions, we make and carefully record observations, make predictions, identify and control variables, measure, make inferences, and communicate our findings. Additional skills may be called upon, depending on the nature of our questions. In this way, science is a verb, involving active manipulation of materials and careful thinking. Science is dependent on language, math, and reading skills, as well as the specialized thinking skills associated with identifying and solving problems.

BASIC PROCESS SKILLS:

Classifying: Grouping, ordering, arranging, or distributing objects, events, or information into categories based on properties or criteria, according to some method or system.

> Example – Using a magnet to sort a set of objects according to their magnetic properties. Testing a set of objects to determine their status as conductors or insulators.

Observing: Using the senses (or extensions of the senses) to gather information about an object or event.

> Example – Seeing and describing the setup of several circuits and noting the differences in a series circuit and a parallel circuit.

Measuring: Using both standard and nonstandard measures or estimates to describe the dimensions of an object or event. Making quantitative observations.

> Example – Using a magnet, several paper clips, and a ruler to determine the relative strength of a magnet.

Inferring: Making an interpretation or conclusion, based on reasoning, to explain an observation.

> Example – Interpreting where the hidden circuits might be in a circuit card or inferring as to where the circuits are in the classroom walls.

Communicating: Communicating ideas through speaking or writing. Students may share the results of investigations, collaborate on solving problems, and gather and interpret data, both orally and in writing. Using graphs, charts, and diagrams to describe data.

> Example – Describing an event or a set of observations; participating in brainstorming and hypothesizing before an investigation; formulating initial and follow-up questions in the study of a topic; summarizing data, interpreting findings, and offering conclusions; questioning or refuting previous findings; making decisions; using graphs to show the relative strength of several magnets.

Science Process Skills (cont.)

Predicting: Making a forecast of future events or conditions in the context of previous observations and experiences.

> Example – Predicting the relative strength of an electromagnet, based on the number of winds around an iron core (nail).

Manipulating Materials: Handling or treating materials and equipment skillfully and effectively.

> Example – Arranging equipment and materials needed to conduct an investigation, then using the materials to set up a series circuit and a parallel circuit.

Replicating: Performing acts that duplicate demonstrated symbols, patterns, or procedures.

> Example – Setting up a simple demonstration electric motor using the diagrams, directions, and materials provided.

Using Numbers: Applying mathematical rules or formulas to calculate quantities or determine relationships from basic measurements.

> Example – Computing the relative strength of an electromagnet relative to the voltage used in the system.

Developing Vocabulary: Specialized terminology and unique uses of common words in relation to a given topic need to be identified and given meaning.

> Example – Using context clues, working definitions, glossaries or dictionaries, word structure (roots, prefixes, suffixes), and synonyms and antonyms to clarify meaning.

Questioning: Questions serve to focus inquiry, determine prior knowledge, and establish purposes or expectations for an investigation. An active search for information is promoted when questions are used. Questioning may also be used in the context of assessing student learning.

> Example – Using what is already known about a topic or concept to formulate questions for further investigation, hypothesizing and predicting prior to gathering data, or formulating questions as new information is acquired.

Using Cues: Key words and symbols convey significant meaning in messages. Organizational patterns facilitate comprehension of major ideas. Graphic features clarify textual information.

> Example – Listing or underlining words and phrases that carry the most important details, or relating key words together to express a main idea or concept.

Science Process Skills (cont.)

INTEGRATED PROCESS SKILLS

Creating Models: Displaying information by means of graphic illustrations or other multisensory representations.

> Example – Drawing a graph or diagram, constructing a three-dimensional object, using a digital camera to record an event, constructing a chart or table, or producing a picture or diagram that illustrates information about the setup of a simple electrical device, such as an electric motor.

Formulating Hypotheses: Stating or constructing a statement that is testable about what is thought to be the expected outcome of an experiment (based on reasoning).

> Example – Making a statement to be used as the basis for an experiment: "The number of objects that can be picked up by an electromagnet is proportionate to the voltage of the system."

Generalizing: Drawing general conclusions from particulars.

> Example – Making a summary statement following analysis of experimental results: "The relative strength of an electromagnet is related to the number of wraps of wire around an iron core."

Identifying and Controlling Variables: Recognizing the characteristics of objects or factors in events that are constant or change under different conditions and that can affect an experimental outcome, keeping most variables constant, while manipulating only one variable.

> Example – Listing or describing the factors that are thought to, or would, influence the flow of current in an electrical circuit.

Defining Operationally: Stating how to measure a variable in an experiment and defining a variable according to the actions or operations to be performed on or with it.

> Example – Defining such things as the strength of an electromagnet in the context of the materials and actions for a specific activity. Hence, the strength of an electromagnet may be measured by finding the number of washers that an electromagnetic system is able to support.

Science Process Skills (cont.)

Recording and Interpreting Data: Collecting bits of information about objects and events that illustrate a specific situation, organizing and analyzing data that has been obtained, and drawing conclusions from it by determining apparent patterns or relationships in the data.

> Example – Recording data (taking notes, making lists/outlines, recording numbers on charts/graphs, tape recordings, photographs, writing numbers of the results of observations/measurements) from the series of experiments to determine the strength of an electromagnet and forming a conclusion that relates trends in data to variables.

Making Decisions: Identifying alternatives and choosing a course of action from among alternatives after basing the judgment for the selection on justifiable reasons.

> Example – Identifying alternative ways to solve a problem through the utilization of a simple electrical circuit; analyzing the consequences of each alternative, such as cost or the effect on other people or the environment; using justifiable reasons as the basis for making choices; choosing freely from the alternatives.

Experimenting: Being able to conduct an experiment, including asking an appropriate question, stating a hypothesis, identifying and controlling variables, operationally defining those variables, designing a "fair" experiment, and interpreting the results of an experiment.

> Example – Utilizing the entire process of designing, building, and testing various electrical devices to solve a problem; arranging equipment and materials to conduct an investigation; manipulating the equipment and materials; and conducting the investigation.

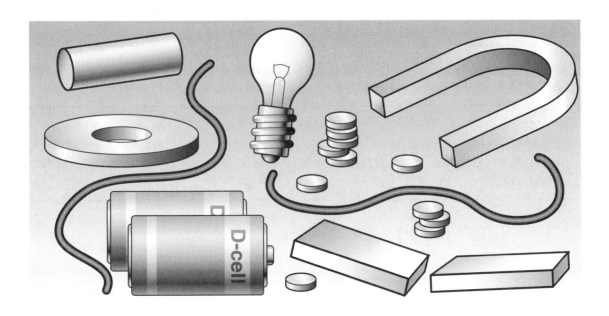

18

Name: _____ Date: _____

Student Inquiry Activity 1 : How An Object Can Become Statically Charged

Topic: Static Electricity

Science, Mathematics, and Technology Standards:
   NSES: Unifying Concepts and Processes; NSES Content Standards (A), (B), (G)
   NCTM: Measurement; Data Analysis and Probability
   STL: Technology and Society; Abilities for a Technological World

Science Concepts:
- Static electricity is electricity at rest, as opposed to current electricity, which flows through a circuit.
- Static charges may be produced through friction.
- Static charges can be transferred through direct contact between two objects, or indirectly by being brought near another object through induction.
- Static charges involve the transfer of electrons from one material to another.

See **Naive Concepts and Terminology Section** for more details.

Science Skills:
   You will make **observations** and **inferences** about the nature of static charge and how materials acquire a charge with simple materials, such as plastic and paper; **estimate** and **measure** the relative strength of electric discharge; make **predictions** and **communicate** with others; **record**, **interpret**, and **analyze data**, **draw general conclusions**; and **make decisions**.

See **Science Process Skills Section** for descriptions and examples.

Materials:
Styrofoam™ packing peanuts broken into smaller pieces or small shreds of paper
Clear plastic containers such as plastic petri dishes or the plastic lids from food containers
A thin plastic bag, such as the bags found in the produce aisles of most grocery stores

Content Background:
   Friction can cause an object to gain a charge. The charged object can then give up a charge through direct contact, or a charge can be induced by bringing the charged object near another material. We experience this sometimes when we walk across a carpet or slide across a car seat and then touch a metal door handle. As we touch the handle, we experience a slight shock as electrons are transferred. An induced charge is experienced when a charged object is brought near another material, and the material responds by moving. For instance, when you rub an inflated balloon on a woolen sweater, and then bring the charged balloon near someone's hair, the hair may respond by standing up straight. In this case, no electrons are transferred between the balloon and the hair; instead, free electrons are being repelled, and the resulting

Name: _____ Date: _____

Student Inquiry Activity 1 : How An Object Can Become Statically Charged (cont.)

positive charge toward the ends of the hair cause it to be attracted to the negatively charged balloon. There are three things to remember: (1) objects can acquire charges through friction; (2) charges (electrons) may be transferred through direct contact with other objects; and (3) a charge may be induced in other objects without contact with no transfer of electrons.

It is important to remember that static electricity demonstrations and experiments work best in dry air. You may have observed that you are more prone to static discharge experiences in the winter, when the relative humidity in indoor spaces is often very low. The reason for this is that charges naturally leak into the air, and humid air will cause the electrons to dissipate even more rapidly.

Challenge Question: How do objects become statically charged?

Procedure:
Put the shredded paper or packing peanuts under the clear plastic lid of a petri dish or food lid. It is best if the plastic lid is no more than 1–2 cm above the shredded material.

A. **Predict** what you think will happen when you rub the plastic lid with the plastic bag.

_____

_____

B. Now **observe** what happens when you rub the lid with a piece of dry plastic bag. Record your observations.

_____

_____

_____

C. In this activity, there are three observable ways in which objects can become charged. What are you doing at the start of the activity that will produce a charge?

_____

_____

Name: _____ Date: _____

Student Inquiry Activity 1 : How An Object Can Become Statically Charged (cont.)

D. What are some other examples of static electricity that you have observed in your daily life?

_____

_____

_____

E. What do you think caused the small bits of foam or paper to be attracted to the lid of the container?

_____

_____

_____

F. How do you think the static environment affects the foam or paper bits? Is there a difference in the charge on the foam pieces on the lid as compared to those still on the table? Explain.

_____

_____

_____

_____

G. Why do some of the pieces of foam or paper fall off the lid?

_____

_____

_____

_____

Conclusions:

H. Explain what you think was happening when you rubbed the plastic lid with the plastic bag.

_____

_____

_____

_____

_____

_____

Name: _____ Date: _____

Student Inquiry Activity 1 : How An Object Can Become Statically Charged (cont.)

I. Explain what you think was happening when the foam or paper bits were moving from the table to the bottom of the lid and back again.

_____

_____

_____

_____

_____

J. What generalizations and tentative conclusions can you make, based on your observations?

_____

_____

_____

_____

_____

Assessment:

1. What are the three ways in which an object can gain a charge? (*Hint:* Note the sequence of events, and this will help you explain how objects can be affected by static charges.)

_____

_____

_____

    Note: The three ways in which objects can become charged are through friction, induction, and conduction.

2. Look at the diagram below and describe the three ways that a charge is produced in the activity.

_____

                         _____

                         _____

                         _____

Name: _____ Date: _____

Student Inquiry Activity **1**: How An Object Can Become Statically Charged (cont.)

Summary:

In this activity, students are observing: (1) **static charge generated through friction** when the plastic bag is rubbed on the plastic lid (the plastic bag removes electrons from the lid, giving the lid a positive charge); (2) **static charge induced** in the small bits of paper or Styrofoam™ peanuts on the table top caused them to jump to the bottom of the lid, because unlike charges attract (the positive plastic lid induces a negative charge on the side of the foam or paper bits toward the lid); and (3) the pieces of foam or paper on the lid slowly lose some of their electrons to the lid through **conduction** and are suddenly repelled by the lid, because like charges repel. The lid maintains a net positive charge, even though it gains some electrons from the small pieces of foam or paper.

Assessment:

Use the following guidelines to assess student performance. Check those statements that apply. The following represent expected responses to questions. The letters correspond to the letters on the student response sheet above.

_____ B. Pieces of Styrofoam™ peanuts or paper jump up and stick to the lid, and some fall back down.

_____ C. The plastic bag was rubbed against the plastic lid to create a charge.

_____ D. Walking on a carpet, sliding across the seat of the car, combing my hair, removing a sweater, clothes rotating in the dryer, etc.

_____ E. The foam or paper pieces are attracted to the lid because they have a different charge. (The charge on the foam or paper is induced by the lid. The lid has a strong positive charge because it has given up electrons to the plastic bag.)

_____ F. The pieces at the top are negative, and the pieces at the bottom are positive.

_____ G. The foam or paper pieces lose some of their electrons to the plastic lid and then are repelled by it as they become positively charged.

Name: _____ Date: _____

Student Inquiry Activity **2** : The Electrophorus and the Lightning Rod or Static Discharge

Topic: Static Electricity

Science Concepts: Static electricity
- The electrophorus is a simple electrostatic generator that depends on an insulator and a conductor.
- Static charges are concentrated at the point of greatest curvature in a material, and if the material has sharp points, electrons may leak off the material into the air.
- A needle may serve as a static electricity arrester when attached to a conducting material by allowing electrons to leak off the conducting material.

See **Naive Concepts and Terminology Section** for more details.

Science Skills:
You will make **observations** and **inferences** about the nature of static charge and discharge in an electrostatic generator called the electrophorus; **estimate** and **measure** the relative strength of electric discharge; make **predictions** and **communicate** with others; **record**, **interpret**, and **analyze data**; **draw general conclusions**; and **make decisions**.

See **Science Process Skills Section** for descriptions and examples.

Materials (per group):
30 centimeter square Styrofoam™ sheet
Piece of woolen cloth
Masking tape
Aluminum pie pan
Styrofoam™ cup
Sewing needle

Content Background:
Electrostatic refers to electric charges that are confined to an object and is called "static electricity" or "electricity at rest." This is in contrast to current electricity, which is electricity that is moving through a circuit. Static charges are developed through friction between two or more objects or materials and may be generated through various means involving friction.

There are several types of electrostatic generators, including the Van de Graaff generator, the Wimshurst machine, and the electrophorus. All three devices produce charges as a result of friction and the migration of electrons within and between materials. The electrophorus is the

Name: _____   Date: _____

Student Inquiry Activity **2** : The Electrophorus and the Lightning Rod or Static Discharge

simplest to set up and use in the classroom. All that is needed is a sheet of Styrofoam™ packing material, a piece of woolen cloth, an aluminum pie pan, and a Styrofoam™ cup.

The Wimshurst machine uses a continuous-acting electrostatic device consisting of two glass disks, with a large number of aluminum strips attached that rotate in opposite directions. As the disks are rotated, the metal strips act to induce and carry a charge. Pointed collector combs pick up and transmit the charges to two Leyden jars that store the charges temporarily.

The Van de Graaff generator consists of a large hollow metal sphere supported by an insulating cylinder. A wide belt made of insulating material runs from a pulley in the base of the generator over a second pulley at the generator's top. The drive pulley and belt are propelled by a motor, and the friction of the belt against a brush at the base of the generator causes a build-up of electrons on the belt. The electrons are picked up at the top of the generator by a second brush and transmitted to the metal sphere. The Van de Graaff generator is used in nuclear physics as a particle accelerator.

How the electrophorus works: Rubbing the Styrofoam™ sheet with a piece of wool causes the Styrofoam™ to become charged with electrons at the surface. Since Styrofoam™ is an insulating material, it cannot transfer its electrons to another material. A charge is built up at its surface, and when an aluminum pie pan is placed on the surface of the Styrofoam™, a charge is induced in the pie pan. Note that the pie pan should have a Styrofoam™ cup taped to its center. (See diagram.) The cup acts as an insulating handle, allowing one to pick up the pie pan. Since aluminum is a good conductor, the negative charge at the surface of the Styrofoam™ causes electrons in the pie pan to migrate away from the Styrofoam™ toward the upper surface of the pie pan. If you bring your finger near the pie pan as it sits on the Styrofoam™ sheet, a visible charge will jump a narrow air gap between your finger and the pan as electrons are repelled toward the earth, or grounded. If the pan is then lifted off the foam sheet by its Styrofoam™ cup handle, and a hand is once again brought near the edge of the pan, a second discharge may be observed as the electrons return to the aluminum pan through air from the finger. Theoretically, this may be repeated over and over again without much electrical charge loss from the Styrofoam™ base.

The lightning rod: After students have experienced the discharge of electrons from and to the pie pan, they are asked to add a sewing needle to the edge of the pie pan, with the point of the needle pointing out. The needle acts as a lightning rod, causing the electrons to discharge into the air.

Benjamin Franklin invented the lightning rod, which is often used to protect wooden buildings from lightning damage. Lightning rods are attached to a building's highest point and connected to the ground by a thick wire, which transfers electrons from the ground to the sky. Sharp-pointed conductors, such as lightning rods, allow electrons to escape from a building's outer surfaces to the sky, instead of through the building. Hence, the pie pan does not build up an observable charge. It is noted that the accumulation of charge in an object is greatest at the points of greatest curvature, so the largest discharges should be observed at the edges of the pie pan. A needle taped to the edge of the pie pan will further concentrate the charge and allow

Name: _____ Date: _____

Student Inquiry Activity 2: The Electrophorus and the Lightning Rod or Static Discharge (cont.)

electrons to escape more readily.

A glowing discharge of energy is often observed on the tips of ships' masts at night and on the trailing edges of airplane wings. Airplane wings are often equipped with pointed masts off the trailing edges of the wings to help remove the charge that the airplanes acquire in flight.

Benjamin Franklin conducted his famous kite experiment with lightning in June of 1752, approximately 250 years ago. He established a theoretical framework for the nature of electricity and electric charge.

Challenge Question: What is an electrophorus, and how does it produce an electric charge?

Procedure: Note: Works best on cool, dry days.
1. Make loops of tape, adhesive side out, and secure the Styrofoam™ sheet to your desktop.
2. Tape the Styrofoam™ cup to the inside of the aluminum pie pan to create an insulating handle for the pie pan.
3. Rub the Styrofoam™ sheet rapidly with the piece of woolen cloth. This causes electrons to be transferred from the woolen cloth to the Styrofoam™ sheet. Be sure not to touch the Styrofoam™ sheet with your hand as you are rubbing it.
4. Using the insulated handle, place the aluminum pie pan on the Styrofoam™ sheet.
5. You are now ready to make observations.

A. **Predict** what you think will happen if you bring your finger near the edge of the aluminum pie pan as it sits on the Styrofoam™ sheet.

    _____

    _____

B. Now **observe** what happens when you touch the edge of the aluminum pan. Record your observations.

    _____

    _____

    _____

Name: _____ Date: _____

Student Inquiry Activity 2 : The Electrophorus and the Lightning Rod or Static Discharge (cont.)

C. After touching the pie pan and observing the results of this action, touch the pan a second and third time. What do you observe?

_____

_____

_____

D. **Predict** what you think will happen if you bring your finger near the edge of the aluminum pie pan when you lift the aluminum pan off the Styrofoam™ sheet.

_____

_____

_____

E. Now, use the Styrofoam™ cup handle to lift the aluminum pan off the Styrofoam™ sheet. Touch the edge of the aluminum pan again. What do you observe?

_____

_____

_____

F. After touching the raised pie pan and observing the results of this action, touch the pan a second and third time. What do you observe?

_____

_____

_____

G. Replace the aluminum pan on the Styrofoam™ sheet and touch it again. What do you observe?

_____

_____

H. Repeat step E and step G several times. What do you observe?

_____

_____

_____

Name: _____ Date: _____

Student Inquiry Activity 2 : The Electrophorus and the Lightning Rod or Static Discharge (cont.)

I. **Predict** what you think will happen when you attach a sewing needle to the edge of the aluminum pan and then bring your finger near the edge of the aluminum pan as it sits on the Styrofoam™ sheet.

_____

_____

_____

J. Use a piece of masking tape to attach a sewing needle to the edge of the aluminum pan, with the sharp end of the needle pointing out. Rub the Styrofoam™ sheet with the woolen cloth and repeat steps B and E. What do you observe?

_____

_____

_____

Conclusions:

1. Why is it important to handle the aluminum pan with the cup handle?

_____

_____

_____

2. Explain what you think was happening when you touched the aluminum pan on the sheet and then touched it again when it was raised?

_____

_____

_____

_____

3. Explain what you think was happening when you touched the aluminum pan on the sheet and then touched it again when it was raised with the needle attached?

_____

_____

_____

_____

Name: _____ Date: _____

Student Inquiry Activity 2 : The Electrophorus and the Lightning Rod or Static Discharge (cont.)

4. What generalizations and tentative conclusions can you make based on your observations?

_____

_____

_____

_____

Summary:

What is being observed in this activity is the transfer of electrons from the aluminum pan through the hand and toward the ground, and the return of the electrons from the hand to the aluminum pan. The electrophorus demonstrates several concepts related to static electricity, including conservation of electrons, the induction of a static charge, and the transfer of electrons from one material to another. Note that the Styrofoam™ sheet gains electrons from the wool but doesn't lose the electrons to the aluminum pan. Instead, the negative charges on the surface of the Styrofoam™ repel the electrons already present in the aluminum pan. The electrons in the aluminum pan migrate to the surface and out to the edges of the pan. Since the Styrofoam™ sheet doesn't lose its charge, it can induce the charge in the aluminum pan over and over again.

The addition of the needle to the aluminum pan demonstrates the effects of adding a lightning rod to the system. There is a concentration of electrons in sharply curved areas in a building or object on the ground; if the area comes to a sharp point, some electrons may drain off into the air. This draining of electrons off a structure offers some protection from lightning strikes during thunderstorms.

Real-World Application:

Static electricity is evident all around us, with lightning representing nature's most powerful display of static electricity. Lightning rods are useful devices for offering some protection to buildings from the effects of lightning strikes.

The rubber tires on a car rubbing against the pavement as the car is in motion will create a static charge on the vehicle. A person riding in the car will pick up a similar charge. When the person exits the car, they may experience a shock, due to the fact that they are making contact with the ground. Similarly, a gasoline can being carried in a car may also pick up the charge from the car's motion. Therefore, a gasoline can should be removed from the vehicle and set on the ground before filling the can. This simple act will serve to discharge any static charge on the can, and reduce the risk of a static spark igniting gasoline fumes in the can.

29

Name: _____ Date: _____

Student Inquiry Activity 2 : The Electrophorus and the Lightning Rod or Static Discharge (cont.)

Assessment:

The Electrophorus

Use the assessment rubric below to evaluate student performance in this activity. Check those statements that apply.

1. _____ The electrophorus is set up correctly.

2. **Student observations**

_____ Observation in B is that a spark is observed.

_____ Observation in C is that no spark is observed with continued touching.

_____ Observation in E is that a spark is observed.

_____ Observation in F is that no spark is observed.

_____ Observation in G is that a spark is observed.

_____ Observation in H is that sparks are observed when the pan is touched in each position, on the Styrofoam™ sheet and off.

_____ Observation in J is that no sparks are observed in either position.

3. **Conclusions**

_____ Students conclude that the handle serves as an insulator.

_____ Students conclude that electrons are transferred from the aluminum pie pan to the finger when the pan is sitting on the Styrofoam™ sheet, and from the finger to the aluminum pan when the pan is raised.

_____ Students conclude that the needle affects the ability of the aluminum pan to transfer electrons.

4. **Generalizations**

_____ Students generalize that the electrophorus demonstrates the conservation of electrons, since they are not lost, but may be transferred from one conductor to another.

_____ Students generalize that a lightning rod may be effective in protecting a building from lightning strikes.

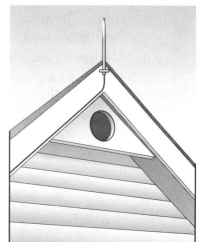

Name: _____   Date: _____

Student Inquiry Activity 3 : Magnetic Field

Topic: Magnetism

Science, Mathematics, and Technology Standards:
NSES: Unifying Concepts and Processes; NSES Content Standards (A), (B), (G)
NCTM: Measurement; Data Analysis and Probability
STL: Technology and Society; Abilities for a Technological World

---

Science Concepts: Magnetism
- Materials may be classified as magnetic or nonmagnetic.
- A magnetic field is a region near a magnetic force or pole that can influence other magnetic materials.
- Lines of force in a magnetic field can be visualized with a magnetic material, such as iron filings scattered over one or both poles of a magnet.

See **Naive Concepts and Terminology Section** for more details.

Science Skills:
You will make **observations** and **inferences** about the nature of a magnetic field at each pole of a magnet, as well as the field that exists between unlike poles and two like poles; **estimate** and **measure** the relative strength of a magnetic field; make **predictions** and **communicate** with others; **record**, **interpret**, and **analyze data**; **draw general conclusions**; and **make decisions**.

See **Science Process Skills Section** for descriptions and examples.

Materials (per group):
2 bar magnets
Iron filings (Note: Pieces of steel wool may be used in place of iron filings.)
Plastic sandwich bag
Styrofoam™ square (example: cut a 1 cm by 1 cm square from a Styrofoam™ egg carton)
Sewing needle
Rectangular or circular plastic container

Content Background:
Magnetic materials are naturally found in the form of an iron ore called **magnetite**. The earth also acts as a giant magnet. The north magnetic pole of the earth is not in the same location as the earth's geographic north pole (axis of rotation). A suspended piece of magnetite will align itself with the magnetic poles of the earth. The alignment of a magnetic material, such as magnetite, with the earth's magnetic poles is an example of the influence of a magnetic field. A magnetic material placed near a magnet will be influenced by that magnet. The region around a magnet that influences magnetic materials is called a **magnetic field**. Theoretically, magnetic influence is mutual, with the stronger field dominating. The path taken by the motion of a magnetic

Name: _____ Date: _____

Student Inquiry Activity 3: Magnetic Field (cont.)

material in a magnetic field is called a **line of flux**, or line of force. The line of force indicates the direction of the magnetic field. The lines of force collectively are called the **magnetic field**.

A magnetic field can be observed in a number of ways. A magnetic compass can be used to estimate the magnetic field, a suspended magnet can be used as an indicator of the influence of the earth's magnetic field, and iron filings can be used to show the magnetic field near a magnet, or between magnets.

Part One

Challenge Question: How can we see the influence of a magnetic field?

Procedure:

1. You will need to magnetize a sewing needle by stroking it along a bar magnet in one direction. Push the magnetized needle through the Styrofoam™ sheet so it is perpendicular to the plastic container.
2. Fill a plastic container (approximately 8 cm by 16 cm) with enough water so the needle floats vertically in the water.

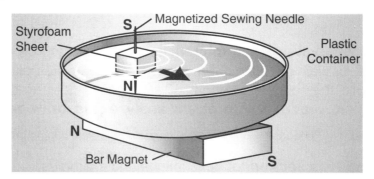

A. Set the plastic container with the floating needle over a bar magnet. Move the needle to the center of the container over the center of the bar magnet. Move the needle to different positions and observe. Rotate the bar magnet and try the needle in different positions. Record your observations.

_____

_____

_____

B. The direction of movement that is being observed in the needle represents a line of force (line of flux). Draw a diagram of the bar magnet and show the lines of force you observe.

Name: _____ Date: _____

Student Inquiry Activity 3 : Magnetic Field (cont.)

C. Measure how far away from the bar magnet the force appears to extend. Record your measurement.

_____

Part Two

Challenge Question: How can you see a magnetic field?

Procedure:

A. Place a bar magnet in a plastic sandwich bag and lay it on a table. Place a piece of paper over the magnet in the plastic bag. Sprinkle iron filings over the paper on top of the plastic bag containing the magnet. Tap the paper. Record your observations by drawing a diagram of the bar magnet and the observed pattern of iron filings.

┌───┐
│   │
│   │
│   │
│   │
│   │
│   │
└───┘

B. The observed pattern represents the magnetic field for the magnet. How far away from the magnet does the field extend? Measure and record this distance.

_____

C. Where do most of the iron filings go?

_____

_____

D. How are your observations with the iron filings related to the floating needle?

_____

_____

_____

E. How does the observed pattern with the iron filings compare to the distance that the needle is attracted to the magnet?

_____

_____

_____

Name: _____ Date: _____

Student Inquiry Activity 3: Magnetic Field (cont.)

F. How can a magnet attract the needle or the iron filings without touching them?

_____

_____

G. What appears to be the strongest part of the magnet?

_____

H. How could you use your iron filings to determine if other materials show a magnetic field?

_____

_____

_____

Conclusions:

I. Magnetic field lines can be used to study the direction of magnetic force and its relative strength. The magnetic field can also be used to determine the extent of the force. Based on your observations, what tentative conclusions can be made about the shape and extent of a magnetic field around a bar magnet?

_____

_____

_____

Extensions:

1. Now that you have explored the magnetic field of one magnet, try two or more magnets. What does the magnetic field look like between two south poles, two north poles, or between a north pole and a south pole?
2. Compare different magnets and their fields. Can you use your iron filings to determine the relative strength of different magnets?
3. Can you determine whether or not the magnetic field is three-dimensional? Does the field extend above and below the magnet, as well as around it?

Summary:

Anyone who has held two magnets in his or her hands and explored their interaction has felt the force that exists around magnets. This force through a distance is called the **magnetic field**. This invisible force exists around every magnet, and can be observed by using iron filings. The space around a magnet where a magnet exerts a force is called a **magnetic field**. It is noted that the lines of force that appear when the iron filings align themselves with the magnet's poles form semi-circles, with the filings aligning north and south. The iron filings have become tiny magnets through induction. Note that the lines of force running from the north to the south poles do not cross over each other.

34

Name: _____ Date: _____

Student Inquiry Activity 3 : Magnetic Field (cont.)

Real-World Application:

Magnetic attraction and magnetic fields have wide-ranging applications, including use in door closers, refrigerator door gaskets, motors, generators, etc.

Assessment: Magnetic Field (Part Two)

Use the assessment rubric below to evaluate student performance in this activity. Check those statements that apply. The following represent expected responses to questions. The letters correspond to the letters on the student response sheet above.

_____ A. The diagram of the magnetic field showing the iron filings over the bar magnet approximates the expected result. See diagram below.

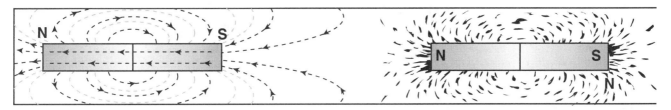

_____ B. Student shows accurate measurements of the magnetic field.

_____ C. Student responses include the observations that most of the filings go to the ends of the magnet, with many lining up between the north and south pole, and that they line up in semi-circles, with their ends aligning with the north and south poles.

_____ D. The floating needle floats toward the poles in paths similar to the lines formed by the magnetized iron filings.

_____ E. The distance in which the floating needle moves is similar to the distance that the iron filings are aligned. The student may observe that the needle is affected a little farther away from the magnet than the iron filings; this is because there is less friction with the water.

_____ F. Because there is a magnetic field around that magnet, and the needle and iron filings are magnetic materials, there is a magnetic field around the magnet, and the magnetic force acts in this area.

_____ G. The strongest parts of the magnet are at each end where the north and south poles are located and the area in the center between the poles.

_____ H. By sprinkling iron filings around other objects to determine if a magnetic field is present.

_____ I. Magnetic field lines formed by iron filings represent one way to study magnetic fields around a magnet. The iron filings can help to determine the strength and direction of the magnetic field and the size of that field. The shape of the field appears to show concentric rings extending from pole to pole and outward from the poles.

Name: _____ Date: _____

Student Inquiry Activity 4: Measuring Magnetic Force—How Much, How Far, and How Thick?

Topic: Magnetism

Science, Mathematics, and Technology Standards:
NSES: Unifying Concepts and Processes; NSES Content Standards
Students should develop the …
(A) Abilities necessary to conduct scientific inquiry and understandings about scientific inquiry
Students should develop an understanding of the …
(B) Properties and changes in properties of matter, motions and forces, and transfer of energy
All students should develop an understanding of …
(G) Science as a human endeavor, the nature of science, and the history of science
NCTM: Measurement; Data Analysis and Probability
STL: Technology and Society; Abilities for a Technological World

---

Science Concepts: Magnetism
- Materials may be classified as magnetic or nonmagnetic.
- Magnetic force is associated with the motion of electric charges and can be measured indirectly by finding out how many similar objects a magnet can pick up.
- Magnetic force can be measured by observing the distance that it attracts magnetic materials.
- Magnetic force is increased as magnets are combined.

See **Naive Concepts and Terminology Section** for more details.

Science Skills:
You will make **observations** and **inferences** about the nature of magnetic force at each pole; **estimate** and **measure** the relative strength of a magnetic force by finding out how many similar objects a magnet can pick up and measure the distance that the magnetic force begins to attract an object; make **predictions** and **communicate** with others; **record**, **interpret**, and **analyze data**; **draw general conclusions**; and **make decisions**.

See **Science Process Skills Section** for descriptions and examples.

Materials (per group):
4–8 rubberized magnets
25–50 paper clips
Centimeter ruler
Various materials for Activity 3, such as textbooks, wood sheets, glass plates, plastic, etc.

Name: _____ Date: _____

Student Inquiry Activity 4: Measuring Magnetic Force—How Much, How Far, and How Thick? (cont.)

Content Background:

Students will conduct three separate but related investigations concerning magnetic attraction and force in this activity. First, they will determine how many objects a magnet can hold and then add magnets to determine if the additional magnets alter the overall magnetic force in the system. Second, they will measure the distance that the magnetic force works through with one magnet. They will also measure the distance that a paper clip will move toward a magnet. They will then add magnets to determine if the distance that the paper clip moved is affected. In the third activity, they will investigate the ability of a magnet to work through various materials. Students can compare materials, such as paper, wood, glass, and metal, to determine if magnetic force passes through each of these materials. They can then measure the effectiveness of magnetic force through materials of varied thicknesses.

In these activities, students can try different kinds of magnets, including bar magnets, ring magnets, ceramic magnets, horseshoe magnets, etc. They will find that magnetic force varies greatly and is not necessarily related to the size of the magnet.

When magnets are combined, the new combination acts as one magnet with an observable increase in force. Students might try to determine whether the new force is equal to two separate magnets. They may also attempt to determine the limits of the new force by continuing to add magnets. For instance, are four magnets twice as strong as two magnets, etc.?

Part One: How Much?

Challenge Question: How many paper clips will a magnet hold?

Procedure:

1. Form a hook with one of the paper clips and let the magnetic force hold the paper clip hook along the side of the magnet. (See diagram at the right.)
2. Predict how many paper clips you think the magnet will hold.
3. Carefully place paper clips on the hook until the system fails. Repeat this three times, recording your data in the table provided.
4. Repeat with two magnets, then three. Make your predictions first, and then proceed with three trials for each setup. Be sure to record the data in the table.
5. Average and analyze the results in each case.
6. Compare your results with the rest of the class.

Set up your magnet(s) and paper clips as in the diagram at the right.

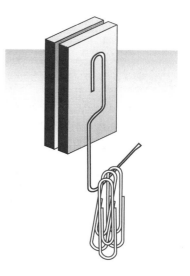

Name: _____ Date: _____

Student Inquiry Activity 4 : Measuring Magnetic Force—How Much, How Far, and How Thick? (cont.)

A. How many paper clips will the magnet(s) hold?

	1 magnet	2 magnets	3 magnets
Predict the number of paper clips that the magnet(s) will hold.			
1st trial			
2nd trial			
3rd trial			
Average number			

B. Summary of your data. _____

_____

_____

Conclusions:

Magnetic force measurements could be used to compare the relative strength of different types of magnets. Based on your observations, what tentative conclusions can be made about the force exerted by the different magnet combinations in this investigation?

_____

_____

_____

Extensions:

1. Now that you have explored the magnetic force of one, two, and three magnets, try several different types of magnets.
2. Compare different magnets and their force. Can you use your paper clips to determine the relative strength of different magnets?

Summary:

Magnets are made of many different materials including iron and iron alloys. The force that a magnet exerts is dependent on many variables, including the condition of the magnet, the inherent alignment of the magnetic domains that exist within it, its material make-up, etc.

Name: _____ Date: _____

Student Inquiry Activity 4 : Measuring Magnetic Force—How Much, How Far, and How Thick? (cont.)

Part Two: How Far?

Challenge Question: What is the distance a magnet can move a paper clip?

Procedure:
1. Predict the distance at which a paper clip will be attracted to a magnet.
2. Place a magnet at one end of a plastic or wooden centimeter ruler and place a paper clip on the ruler. Slowly slide the paper clip toward the magnet until the magnet attracts the paper clip. Record the distance in centimeters that represents a measure of magnetic force.
3. Repeat this three times, recording your data in the table provided.
4. Repeat with two magnets, and then three magnets. Make your predictions first, and then proceed with three trials for each setup. Be sure to record the data in the table.
5. Average and analyze the results in each case.
6. Compare your results with the rest of the class.

   Set up your magnet(s), ruler, and paper clip according to the diagram below.

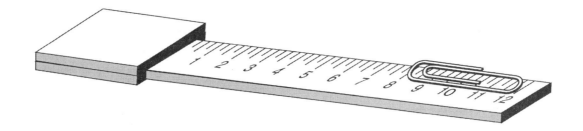

A. What distance is observed for the magnetic force on a paper clip?

	1 magnet	2 magnets	3 magnets
Predict the distance that a paper clip moves.			
1st trial			
2nd trial			
3rd trial			
Average distance			

Name: _____ Date: _____

Student Inquiry Activity 4: Measuring Magnetic Force—How Much, How Far, and How Thick? (cont.)

B. Summary of your data. _____

_____

_____

_____

Conclusions:

Magnetic force measurements could be used to compare the relative strength of different types of magnets. Based on your observations, what tentative conclusions can be made about the force exerted by the different magnet combinations in this investigation?

_____

_____

_____

_____

Summary:

The force that a magnet exerts and its accompanying magnetic field is dependent on many variables, including the condition of the magnet and the inherent alignment of the magnetic domains that exist within it, its material makeup, etc. The distance that is observed represents the extent of the magnetic force; however, the magnetic force may extend beyond what is observed. Factors such as friction may affect your observations. It is advisable to think of your findings as representing an estimate of the observable magnetic field in each case.

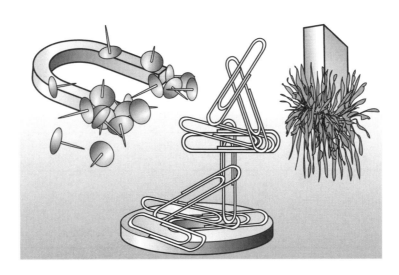

Name: _____ Date: _____

Student Inquiry Activity 4: Measuring Magnetic Force—How Much, How Far, and How Thick? (cont.)

Part Three: How Thick?

Challenge Questions: Will a magnet attract a paper clip through materials? If so, through what thickness will the magnet show its force?

Procedure:

1. **Part A:** Test various materials, such as paper, wood, plastic, glass, and metal, to see if a magnet or magnets will attract a paper clip. You may test through your desk top, a door in the classroom, a glass window pane, a textbook, plastic storage boxes, etc.
   Part B: After testing several different types of materials to determine if magnetic force will work through them, measure the thickness through which magnetic force is observable.
2. Record your findings in Part A in the blanks provided.
3. Record your data from Part B in the table provided.
4. Repeat with two magnets, then three. Make your predictions first, and then test each material. Be sure to record the data in the table.
5. Analyze the results.
6. Compare your results to those of the rest of the class.

   Set up your magnet(s), the material being tested, centimeter ruler, and paper clip according to the diagram below.

Name: _____ Date: _____

Student Inquiry Activity 4: Measuring Magnetic Force—How Much, How Far, and How Thick? (cont.)

Part A:

Will magnetism work through …?

If possible, compare materials that are similar in thickness. Note: Do not test magnetic media such as CDs, DVDs, etc.

	Prediction	**Test Results**
Paper		
Wood		
Plastic		
Metal		

A. Summary of your findings for the materials tested.

_____

_____

_____

_____

_____

Part B:

Through what thickness will the magnet show its force?

1. Record the name of the material being tested in the first box of each row.
2. Record the measured thickness that a magnetic force was observed in the boxes for one, two, and three magnets for each material.

Name: _____ Date: _____

Student Inquiry Activity 4: Measuring Magnetic Force—How Much, How Far, and How Thick? (cont.)

	1 magnet	2 magnets	3 magnets
Predict the thickness through which a paper clip will be moved by a magnetic force.			
1st material tested:			
2nd material tested:			
3rd material tested:			
4th material tested:			

B. Summary of your data.

_____

_____

_____

_____

_____

_____

Conclusions:

Magnetic force measurements could be used to compare the relative strength of different types of magnets. Based on your observations, what tentative conclusions can be made about the force exerted by the different magnet combinations in this investigation?

Summary:

A magnet's force acts through space, and certain materials appear to be relatively transparent to a magnetic field. Students may observe that magnetic materials such as iron or steel will interrupt or block the magnetic force. The iron or steel is said to "cut" the magnetic field. Hence, iron or steel is a material that may be used to shield objects from a magnetic field.

A magnetic field extends beyond the ends of a magnet. Magnets send out lines of force through space to attract materials. It is assumed that air is a material that we can add to the list of substances that magnetic force will act through.

Name: _____ Date: _____

Student Inquiry Activity 5 : The Compass and the Earth's Magnetic Field

Topic: The Earth's Magnetic Field

Science, Mathematics, and Technology Standards

NSES: The Unifying Concepts in Science, including: Systems, order, and organization; Evidence, models, and explanation; and Change, constancy, and measurement. Content Standard A (inquiry), Standard D (earth and space science), Standard F (science in personal and social perspectives), and Standard G (history and nature of science)

NCTM: Measurement

STL: Technology and Society; Abilities for a Technological World

See **National Standards Section** for more information on each standard.

Science Concepts:

Every magnet has two poles; one pole is referred to as the north pole, and the other is called the south pole. The earth acts as a giant magnet, complete with a north pole and a south pole. A freely suspended magnet will align itself with the earth's magnetic poles. The pole that points to the earth's north pole is called the north pole, and the pole that points to the earth's south pole is called the south pole. It is an accepted convention in science to refer to the end of a freely swinging magnet pointing to the earth's north pole as the "north-seeking pole," or simply the north pole of the magnet. A compass is a freely suspended magnet, usually in the form of a magnetized needle, that will align itself with the earth's poles.

Science Skills:

You will make **observations** and **inferences** about the nature of the earth's magnetic field and the interaction of a magnet with that field. A **model** of the earth showing its inferred magnetic field can be created using information from observing a magnetic field around a simple magnet.

Materials:

Bar magnet
Plastic tub or glass pan (non-metallic container)
Styrofoam™ or plastic plate (diameter must be longer than the length of the bar magnet and small enough to fit in a pan of water)
Magnetic compass

Content Background:

The compass has had a great impact on the human history of the earth. The invention of the compass and its use as a navigational device impacted trade, commerce, and the world's human migration patterns. Natural magnetic material called lodestone (leading stone) was known to the Chinese as early as 800 B.C., and they apparently invented the compass around the first century A.D. (Aczel, 2001). Aczel, in *The Riddle of the Compass,* recounts the story of a Chinese

Name: _____ Date: _____

Student Inquiry Activity 5 : The Compass and the Earth's Magnetic Field (cont.)

emperor's palace that in 806 B.C. included giant magnetic gates that were used to detect concealed iron weapons carried by anyone passing through the gates. This may represent the first magnetic security gate used by humans (Aczel, p.79).

This activity is intended to show that any magnet can be used to demonstrate that the earth is a giant magnet.

Challenge Question: How can a magnet be used to locate the North Pole?

Procedure:
1. Fill the glass pan or plastic tub with enough water to float the Styrofoam™ plate.
2. Place a bar magnet on the floating plate.
3. Allow the plate to stop moving, and observe the orientation of the bar magnet. It may be necessary to periodically move the plate away from the side of the pan or tub.

4. After the plate has stopped moving, observe how the magnet has aligned itself.

5. Use the magnetic compass to determine in which directions (north-south; east-west; northeast-southwest, etc.) the bar magnet points. In which direction is the bar magnet pointing?

_____

6. Rotate the plate with the bar magnet on it and allow it to turn freely again. Do the bar magnet and plate spin to point in the same direction as before?

_____

Conclusions:
1. Explain why the bar magnet always pointed the same way.

_____

_____

_____

_____

45

Name: _____ Date: _____

Student Inquiry Activity 5 : The Compass and the Earth's Magnetic Field (cont.)

2. Explain why the container holding the water should be made of either plastic or glass.

_____

_____

_____

Summary:

1. Summarize your findings by drawing a diagram of the earth on your own paper, showing its magnetic field. How is knowledge of the earth's magnetic field used with the compass for navigation?

_____

_____

_____

_____

Extensions

1. Try other magnets and pieces of lodestone on the Styrofoam™ plate, and make your own magnetic materials for testing your inferences about the earth's magnetic field.

Real-World Applications

Magnetic compasses, used by many different professionals, such as surveyors, navigators, hikers, and so on, use the same principle as demonstrated in this activity. Oftentimes, more sophisticated compasses are encased in a liquid-filled housing. The liquid acts as a dampening agent, allowing the compass needle to move freely but also more slowly and more smoothly.

Assessment:

1. Explain how you could determine which direction north is by using a horseshoe magnet and a small straight pin.

_____

_____

_____

_____

_____

_____

Name: _____ Date: _____

Student Inquiry Activity 6 : The Electromagnet

Topic: Electromagnetism – This activity shows that when a current of electricity is flowing through a coil of insulated wire wrapped around an iron core, it acts as a magnet.

Science, Mathematics, and Technology Standards:
  NSES: The Unifying Concepts in Science, including: Systems, order, and organization; Evidence, models, and explanation; and Change, constancy, and measurement. Content Standard A (inquiry), Standard B (physical science, transfer of energy), Standard E (science and technology), and Standard G (history and nature of science)
  NCTM: Measurement
  STL: Technology and society; abilities for a technological world

(See **National Standards Section** for more information on each standard.)

Science Concepts:

   Current electricity is represented by the flow of electrons through a conducting material such as wire. In order for electricity to flow through a conducting wire, a circuit must be established. That is, the electricity must originate from an energy source, such as a battery, and move through a closed or complete circuit back to the energy source. The word *circuit* has as its root *circa* or *circle*. Visualizing a circle that includes a battery as an energy source, a wire as a conductor, and perhaps a light bulb as an appliance, is an example of a simple complete or closed circuit.

   A coil of insulated wire wrapped around an iron core acts as a temporary magnet when the ends of the wire are connected to a battery. The iron core is magnetized through induction by the magnetic field that surrounds the insulated wire.

Science Skills:

   You will make **observations** and **inferences** about the creation of a magnetic field through induction in a coil of wire around an iron nail. You will **measure** the relative strength of the electromagnet by making **observations** on how many paper clips the electromagnet is able to pick up. You can also compare the relative strengths of several different electromagnets and **record and analyze the data** using data tables and graphs.

Materials: (per student or group of students)
2 D-cell batteries   2 battery holders
1 piece of insulated bell wire, 1 meter long   1 large iron nail
1 box of small paper clips

Content Background:

   This activity gives you an opportunity to explore the relationship between electricity and magnetism, and how an electric circuit can be used to induce a temporary magnetic field in an iron nail. You can explore turning the magnetism on and off by alternately turning an electric circuit on and off and measuring the relative strength of the created electromagnet.

Name: _____ Date: _____

Student Inquiry Activity 6 : The Electromagnet (cont.)

You can also wrap the coil of wire around the nail 5, 10, 15, and 20 times to compare the relative strength of several types of electromagnets.

Electromagnets have many applications, especially where magnetic contact is used to alternately turn an appliance on and off. The electric doorbell is an example of such a use. Pushing a doorbell switch completes an electric circuit that turns on an electromagnet that pulls the bell clapper toward a gong. This action breaks the circuit, turning off the electromagnet. The clapper moves back to a position that completes the circuit, starting the process over again. This cycle is repeated several times each second.

In this activity, you are building a device similar to the cranes that are used to pick up and move scrap metal as pictured below.

Challenge Question: Can you make and test the strength of an electromagnet?

Procedure: (See the diagram on the following page.)
1. Using a piece of insulated wire one meter long and starting about 40 centimeters from one end, wrap the wire tightly around the nail 20 times.
2. Connect the ends of the meter-long wire to two 1.5-volt batteries arranged in series.
3. Touch the pointed end of the nail to a pile of paper clips.
4. Now, try using the nailhead end to pick up the paper clips.
5. In the chart below, record the number of paper clips you were able to pick up with the nail, comparing the pointed end of the nail and the nailhead.
6. Repeat the procedure above with 30 wraps, and then 40 wraps of wire around the nail.

Name: _____ Date: _____

Student Inquiry Activity 6 : The Electromagnet (cont.)

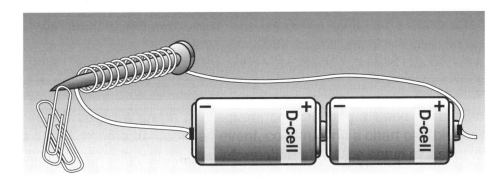

Twenty (20) wraps	Number of paper clips picked up	
	Pointed end of nail	Nailhead
Trial One		
Trial Two		
Trial Three		

Thirty (30) wraps	Number of paper clips picked up	
	Pointed end of nail	Nailhead
Trial One		
Trial Two		
Trial Three		

Forty (40) wraps	Number of paper clips picked up	
	Pointed end of nail	Nailhead
Trial One		
Trial Two		
Trial Three		

Conclusions:

A. What can you infer about the relationship of electricity to magnetism?

_____

_____

_____

_____

Name: _____   Date: _____

Student Inquiry Activity 6: The Electromagnet (cont.)

B. Compare your data for the difference in the effectiveness of the pointed end of the nail to the nailhead for each of the three "wraps" (20, 30, and 40).

_____

_____

_____

C. What happens when you try to pick up paper clips with the wires disconnected?

_____

_____

D. Where is your electromagnet the strongest? _____

_____

E. How is the strength of the magnet increased? _____

_____

F. Hypothesize about some other ways to increase the strength of the electromagnet.

_____

_____

_____

G. What are some advantages of the electromagnet over the permanent magnet?

_____

_____

H. What are some applications or uses for the electromagnet? _____

_____

_____

I. Summarize your findings by making a statement about the relationship of the number of wraps to the strength of an electromagnet.

_____

_____

_____

_____

Name: _____ Date: _____

Student Inquiry Activity 6 : The Electromagnet (cont.)

Summary:

A coil of wire that uses an electric current to make a magnetic field is called an **electromagnet**. This system takes advantage of the relationship between magnetism and electricity. An advantage of an electromagnet over a permanent magnet is that it can be turned on and off, and the strength of the magnetism can be varied.

Extensions:

1. After testing the electromagnet, use a magnetic compass to determine the nature and extent of the magnetic field that exists, if any, around the wire, nail, and battery in this system.

2. Test different materials for the core of the electromagnet, such as a steel bolt, aluminum nail, nails with different diameters, and a pencil.

3. Compare the strength of the empty coil of wire and the coil of wire wrapped around the nail.

4. Test wire by length. Use a piece of wire 75 cm long or a piece 125 cm long. Note that it is also possible to test wire varying in thickness or diameter. However, thin wire can get very hot for students to handle, and thick wire may be difficult to wind around the nail.

5. Using a magnetic compass, test the relationship of the magnetism in the coiled nail to the way that it is connected to the batteries. Reverse the connections on the batteries and bring the coil-covered nail near the magnetic compass; then observe the deflection of the needle in the compass.

Real-World Applications:

Electromagnets are used in everyday items, such as telephone receivers, doorbells, and circuit breakers. Electromagnets are used on the end of crane booms for moving scrap metal. Additionally, electromagnetic sorting machines are used in recycling or separating iron-based materials from other substances. The electric motor also uses an electromagnetic coil to create rotational motion in a shaft or axle. The electric generator or alternator is the opposite of the electric motor, in that rotational motion is used to generate electricity. The telegraph worked as a simple electromagnet.

Name: _____ Date: _____

Student Inquiry Activity 6 : The Electromagnet (cont.)

Assessment:

Use the following guidelines to assess student performance. Check those statements that apply. The following represent expected responses to questions. The letters correspond to the letters on the student response sheet above.

_____ A. A magnetic field is present around the wire of a closed circuit.

_____ B. The two ends of the nail appear to be similar, with the nailhead picking up more paper clips than the pointed end of the nail.

_____ C. The nail is unable to pick up paper clips with the electric circuit open or off.

_____ D. At the ends of the nail. These represent the poles of the magnet. This can be checked using a magnetic compass.

_____ E. The strength of the electromagnet can be increased by adding more wire wraps around the nail.

_____ F. The strength of the electromagnet can be increased by adding more batteries, or by using a thicker nail or bolt.

_____ G. An electromagnet can be turned on and off, and the strength can be varied.

_____ H. Doorbell, telegraph key, telephone receiver, circuit breaker.

_____ I. The greater the number of wraps, the stronger the electromagnet.

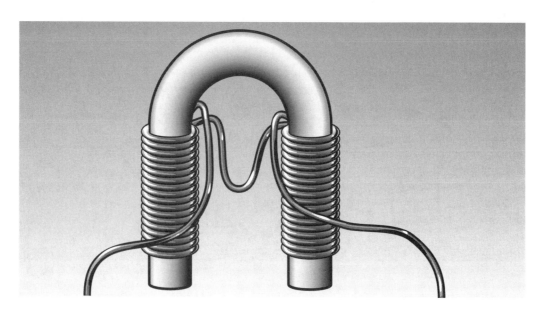

Name: _____   Date: _____

Student Inquiry Activity **7** : Lighting a Bulb

Topic: Battery,   Bulbs, and Electricity

Science, Mathematics, and Technology Standards:
   NSES: The Unifying Concepts in Science, including: Systems, order, and organization; and Evidence, models, and explanation. Content Standard A (inquiry); Standard B (physical science, transfer of energy); and Standard E (science and technology)
   NCTM: Number and Operations; Measurement
   STL: The Nature of Technology; Technology and Society; Design; Abilities for a Technological World

(See **National Standards Section** for more information on each standard.)

Science Concepts:
   An electrical circuit is a complete path through which electrons flow from an energy source, through a conducting wire and appliance, and back to the energy source. A complete circuit may also be called a closed circuit. Switches are used to open and close circuits. An open circuit is off, and a closed circuit is on. Electrical circuits are used to convert electrical energy into light, sound, and heat energy. There are different ways to connect appliances in a circuit.

See **Naive Concepts and Terminology** for more details.

Science Skills:
   You will make **observations** and **inferences** about the flow of electricity in an electrical circuit. You will **create models** of simple circuits using common symbols, and **explain** and **communicate** how the circuits operate.

See **Science Process Skills Section** for descriptions and examples.

Materials:
Bell wire
Flashlight bulbs
Three batteries (preferably D-cell)
(Most school science supply companies carry commercial-type battery- and bulb-holders that may be used in these activities to make it easier for students to manipulate their materials.)

Content Background:
   The movement of electrically charged particles of the atom called **electrons** results in the flow of electricity. In static electricity, charged particles increase in one location (stationary charge). A discharge or movement of electrons occurs when a conductor is brought near a body that has built up a negative or positive "static" charge. This discharge is sudden and may result in a visible spark.

Name: _____   Date: _____

Student Inquiry Activity 7 : Lighting a Bulb (cont.)

In current electricity, these same electrically charged particles are in constant motion through a path called a circuit. In its simplest form, a circuit must contain an energy source or battery and a piece of wire. Most often, the energy source is a dry-cell battery containing different chemicals that continuously react with each other, producing an excess of electrons. Hence, chemical energy is transformed into electrical energy. The chemicals commonly used in batteries are a mixture of ammonium chloride and zinc chloride, in which a carbon rod has been placed. The electrons leave the battery from the negative end of the battery (usually marked with a -) and return to the positive end (usually marked with +) through a wire called a conductor. Along the path of this wire, there may be one or more electrical appliances or devices, such as bulbs, motors, buzzers, etc.

Light bulbs may be of a variety of types, the most common of which is the incandescent bulb. These bulbs typically screw into a light socket. Many homes also use fluorescent light bulbs. These are normally in the shape of a long tube or a circular tube, although recent technology has developed smaller tubes in a number of different shapes. The incandescent bulb contains a small wire called a **filament**. The purpose of the filament is not only to conduct the electrical current but to slow or resist the current's flow. In resisting the current's flow, the filament will heat up. If the filament is in an atmosphere with enough oxygen, the filament will ignite and burn. Incandescent bulbs contain a gas other than oxygen, so when the filament heats up, it does not ignite fully, but instead, glows or burns slowly. This glowing produces light.

Challenge Question: Can you light a bulb using one battery, one piece of wire, and one bulb?

Procedure:

1. Using one light bulb, one battery, and one piece of wire, make the bulb light up.

2. Explain how you were able to make the bulb light up.

    A. Which part of the bulb is the positive end of the battery touching?

    _____

    B. One end of the wire touches the negative end (-) of the battery. Which part of the bulb is the other end of the wire touching?

    _____

Circuits are often shown with diagrams. To make diagrams consistent and easier to understand, electricians use symbols for certain objects. The following are symbols that may be used to represent the electrical components.

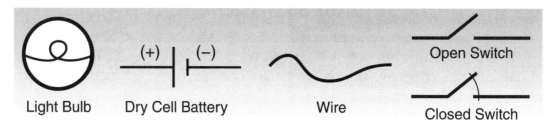

Light Bulb   Dry Cell Battery   Wire   Open Switch / Closed Switch

54

Name: _____ Date: _____

Student Inquiry Activity 7 : Lighting a Bulb (cont.)

C. Draw a picture of how you arranged the battery, wire, and bulb to get the bulb to light.

D. Draw a second way to arrange the light bulb, battery, and wire to make the bulb light up. Test to see if your second way to light the bulb also works.

Are there other ways to light the bulb?

Conclusions:

E. Explain what must happen in order for the bulb to light up.

_____

_____

_____

_____

_____

Name: _____ Date: _____

Student Inquiry Activity 7 : Lighting a Bulb (cont.)

Summary:

In order for a bulb to light up, you need to form a circuit consisting of four contact points. Two of the contact points are on a battery and are called the terminals. One terminal is called the positive terminal and is represented by a "+" sign. The other terminal is called the negative terminal and is represented by a "-" sign. The positive end (+) of the battery is the end with a small knob on the end, and the negative end (-) is usually fairly flat. The bulb also has two contact points; one is the metal side of the bulb, and the other is the silver tip on the bottom of the bulb. Either by direct contact or through the use of wire(s), each end of the battery must be touching one of the points of contact on the bulb to complete the circuit and light the bulb.

Extensions:

1. Carefully wrap a light bulb in a thick cloth or thick layers of paper towel. Then, use a pair of pliers to slowly and gently squeeze the glass part of the light bulb until the glass breaks. Remove the broken glass and examine the bulb's filament. Try lighting the bulb that has had the glass cover removed and observe the results. **Safety goggles and gloves are recommended for this activity. Adults may want to break the light bulbs before the activity begins.**
2. Can you make a bulb light if it is not touching a battery?
3. Can you make a switch?
4. Build a simple circuit with a battery, wires, and a doorbell.

Real-World Applications:

Light bulbs and electrical circuits are used in thousands of ways in our daily lives. Turning on the lights in a room or on a desk requires the use of a circuit. Radios, computers, and nearly all everyday electrical devices use circuits. While the circuits created in this activity are large, today's technology is able to design circuits that are compact and miniature in size.

Assessment:

Use the following guidelines to assess student performance. Check those statements that apply. The following represent expected responses to questions. The letters correspond to the letters on the student response sheet on the previous pages.

_____ A & B. The student's response should indicate that one end of the battery or wire should touch the silver tip at the base of the bulb, and the other end of the battery or wire should touch the metal side of the bulb.

_____ C. The drawing should show the two contact points on the battery touching the two contact points on the bulb.

_____ D. The drawing should be a different arrangement of the four contact points being in contact.

_____ E. The student's concluding statement should indicate that the student understands that there are two points of contact on both the bulb and the battery, and that these points must touch each other to make a working circuit.

56

Name: _____ Date: _____

Student Inquiry Activity 8 : Parallel and Series Circuits

Topic: Parallel and Series Circuits
 This activity is designed to explore the two basic types of circuits, **series** and **parallel**. In the series circuit, appliances, such as light bulbs, are arranged with a single conducting path of current running through all of the light bulbs. In a parallel circuit, each light bulb or appliance is supplied with a separate conducting path for the current.

Science, Mathematics, and Technology Standards
 NSES: The Unifying Concepts in Science, including: Systems, order, and organization; and Evidence, models, and explanation. Content Standard A (inquiry); Standard B (physical science, transfer of energy); and Standard E (science and technology)
 NCTM: Number and Operations; Measurement
 STL: The Nature of Technology; Abilities for a Technological World

(See **National Standards Section** for more information on each standard.)

Science Concepts:
A **circuit** is a continuous path of flowing electrons from an energy source through wires and appliances (resistors) and back to the energy source.
A **parallel circuit** is a circuit with two or more appliances that are connected so as to provide separate conducting paths for current for each appliance.
A **series circuit** is a circuit with two or more appliances that are connected so as to provide a single conducting path for current.
Electricity is the physical attraction and repulsion of electrons within and between materials.

See **Naive Concepts and Terminology** for more details.

Science Skills:
 The student will gather information about circuits through **observations** and **inferences**; will **classify** circuits as either parallel or series; will be able to determine the voltage **measurement** in different circuits; and will create circuits through the **manipulation of materials**.

See **Science Process Skills Section** for descriptions and examples.

Materials (for each group):
3 Batteries (1.5 volts)
3 Flashlight bulbs
Bell wire
Tape (electrical, duct, or masking)
(Most school science supply companies carry commercial-type battery- and bulb-holders that may be used in these activities to make it easier for students to manipulate their materials.)

Name: _____ Date: _____

Student Inquiry Activity 8 : Parallel and Series Circuits (cont.)

Content Background:

In previous activities, you learned that the path through which electricity flows is known as a **circuit**. A basic circuit consists of an energy source and a device or appliance that uses the energy. This device might be a light bulb, motor, or some other type of electrical device. More complex circuits contain more than one device. These multiple devices may be connected in the circuit in either a series or parallel configuration.

When devices are configured in a **series circuit**, the electricity must pass through all the devices once it leaves the energy source and until it returns to the energy source. This type of circuit results in all devices in the circuit failing to function if just one device breaks the circuit or does not work. Older-style strings of Christmas tree lights were in a series circuit; this meant that if one of the lights burned out, the entire string would not operate. This is because the electric current flowed through each bulb, then through the next bulb, and so on. If one bulb burned out, it broke the circuit; then it was necessary to check each bulb in order to find the one that had burned out. Additionally, the electric current is reduced in a series circuit because of the resistance to the flow that occurs in each appliance in the circuit. Hence, the total resistance in a series circuit is equal to the sum of the separate resistances in the circuit.

In a **parallel circuit**, when the electricity leaves the energy source, the electrical energy goes through each appliance through a separate circuit, so that each appliance may operate independently of the other appliances. Strings of modern holiday lights are wired in parallel; therefore, when one bulb burns out, the other bulbs in the circuit remain lit, because each bulb has a separate conducting path for current. Since each bulb in a string of lights wired in parallel has its own circuit, the bulbs in a parallel circuit burn brighter than those in a series circuit.

Light bulbs will become brighter if you add more batteries to the circuit. Batteries may be added to the circuit in either a **series** or in a **parallel** arrangement. The most common method of adding batteries to a circuit is in series, or in a row. This occurs when you connect the positive end of one battery to the negative end of a second battery. By connecting batteries in series, the voltage becomes the sum of the voltages of individual batteries. While household batteries (Types D, B, A, AA, AAA) can come in different sizes, most contain 1.5 volts. If you place two 1.5-volt batteries in a series, the circuit's voltage would be 3.0 volts (1.5 v + 1.5 v = 3.0 v). If you connect three 1.5-volt batteries in series, the circuit's total voltage is 4.5 volts (1.5 v + 1.5 v + 1.5 v = 4.5 v). Therefore, connecting batteries in series will increase the total voltage of the circuit.

Batteries may also be added to a circuit in a parallel arrangement. Batteries arranged in parallel are usually aligned side-by-side, with the positive terminals connected to each other by one wire and the negative terminals connected to each other with a second wire. No matter how many 1.5-volt batteries you connect in parallel, the total output of the circuit is 1.5 volts. Because batteries connected in series will drain each battery equally, the advantage of placing batteries in parallel is that the batteries will last longer.

Challenge Question: How can you make a bulb brighter?

Name: _____ Date: _____

Student Inquiry Activity **8** : Parallel and Series Circuits (cont.)

Procedure
Activity 1. Making a Bulb Brighter

A. In the activity "Lighting a Bulb," you used one battery, one bulb, and one wire to make one bulb light. What could you do to make the bulb brighter? Using the materials provided, modify your circuit so the bulb is brighter.

Explain what you did to make the bulb brighter. Include a diagram of your circuit using the appropriate symbols.

_____

_____

_____

_____

B. If the positive end (+) of the battery in the new circuit touches the negative end (-) of a second battery, then your batteries are arranged in series. If the positive end of one battery is connected to the positive end of a second battery, and the negative ends of the batteries are connected in a similar way, then your batteries are connected in parallel. See the diagrams below to determine what type of circuit you have.

Diagram of batteries in series   Diagram of batteries in parallel

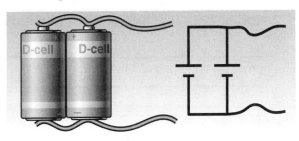

What type of circuit have you created? _____

Name: _____ Date: _____

Student Inquiry Activity 8 : Parallel and Series Circuits (cont.)

C. How does the brightness of the bulb compare to your original circuit with just one bulb and one battery?

_____

_____

D. If the circuit you constructed in Part B was a series circuit, then construct a parallel circuit. If the circuit you constructed in Part B was a parallel circuit, then construct a series circuit.

What type of circuit do you now have? _____

E. How does the brightness of the bulb compare to your original circuit with just one bulb and one battery?

_____

_____

Conclusions:

F. Make a generalization as to the brightness of a bulb when two batteries are connected in series vs. parallel.

_____

_____

_____

To test your generalization, try a series circuit with three batteries and a parallel circuit with three batteries.

Procedure:
Activity 2: Adding More Lights

A. Just like batteries, bulbs in a circuit may be arranged in series or parallel. Construct a circuit with two bulbs. (You may want to use two batteries in series in this circuit.) Once you have your circuit constructed and the bulbs working, disconnect one of the wires touching one of the bulbs. What happens? Are both bulbs still lit? Is one bulb still lit?

_____

_____

_____

Name: _____ Date: _____

Student Inquiry Activity 8 : Parallel and Series Circuits (cont.)

Bulbs may be arranged in a series or parallel circuit. If two bulbs are in series, and one goes out, the other also goes out. If two bulbs are in parallel and one goes out, the other bulb remains lit.

B. Are the bulbs in the circuit you have created in series or parallel?

_____

Below are diagrams of bulbs in a series and bulbs in a parallel circuit. If the parallel or series circuit you have created does not look like the picture, then change your circuit now.

Diagram of bulbs in series

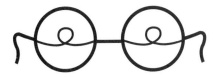

Diagram of bulbs in parallel

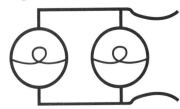

If your circuit is series, disconnect one of the bulbs to see if the other bulb remains lit. If your circuit is parallel, disconnect one of the bulbs to see if the other bulb also goes out.

Now investigate the other type of circuit.

C. How does the brightness of the bulbs compare when in series and when in parallel?

_____

_____

_____

Conclusions:

D. Make a statement that explains what you have learned about bulbs in a series circuit.

_____

_____

_____

E. Make a statement that explains what you have learned about bulbs in a parallel circuit.

_____

_____

_____

Name: _____   Date: _____

Student Inquiry Activity 8 : Parallel and Series Circuits (cont.)

Summary:

Electrical circuits are either series or parallel. Series circuits require the electrical current to flow through all the devices in the circuit in just one path to make a complete circuit. Parallel circuits allow for more than one path along which the current can flow. Therefore, if one path in a parallel circuit has a break in it, the electrical current can still travel through the circuit that allows other devices in the circuit to operate. Because the current must flow through all the devices in a series circuit, the circuit has a higher resistance, and the bulbs in the circuit will be less bright. In a parallel circuit, because the current can flow around openings in the circuit, the resistance is less; therefore, the bulbs in the circuit are brighter.

Extensions:

1. Construct a simple flashlight with a switch. (Suggestion: use a toilet paper tube as the battery holder).

2. Using a box, create a "room" with one light and two doors. Wire the "room" so that the light may be turned on or off from either door.

Real-World Applications:

Obtain an ordinary household flashlight; one that requires two C- or D-type batteries is preferred. Open the flashlight, and then remove the batteries and observe whether they are in parallel or series arrangement. What type of arrangement did you find? How many volts of electricity are produced by this arrangement? Why do you think flashlight manufacturers make flashlights like this?

Name: _____ Date: _____

Student Inquiry Activity 8: Parallel and Series Circuits (cont.)

Assessments:

Use the following guidelines to assess student performance. Check those statements that apply. The following represent expected responses to questions. The letters correspond to the letters on the student response sheet on the previous pages.

Activity 1: Making a Bulb Brighter

_____ A. Student responses should indicate the inclusion of additional batteries to the circuit. Student diagram should include the appropriate symbols.

_____ B. Student should have either a parallel circuit or series circuit. See student's diagram in Part A to determine if the student is correct.

_____ C. If the student has a parallel circuit, the brightness of the bulb will be the same as in the original circuit. If the student has a series circuit, the bulb will be brighter.

_____ D. Student will construct a circuit the opposite of the one constructed in Part B.

_____ E. Again, if student has a parallel circuit, the brightness of the bulb will be the same as in the original circuit. If the student has a series circuit, the bulb will be brighter.

_____ F. Student response should indicate that the bulb will be brighter when two batteries are in series than when two batteries are in parallel.

Activity 2: Adding More Lights

_____ A. Student response will be that either the bulb stays lit, or the bulb goes out, depending on the type of circuit constructed.

_____ B. If, in Part A, the student stated that the bulb goes out, then the circuit is series. If the student stated that the bulb stays lit, then the bulbs are in a parallel circuit.

_____ C. Student response should indicate that the bulbs are brighter in a parallel circuit than in a series circuit.

_____ D. Student response should indicate an understanding that when bulbs are in series and one bulb burns out, then the other bulb stops functioning also.

_____ E. Student response should indicate an understanding that when bulbs are in parallel and one bulb burns out, then the other bulb will continue to be lit.

Name: _____ Date: _____

Student Inquiry Activity 9 : Controlling the Circuit

Topic: Electricity

This activity introduces switches and fuses and the double-pole switch. All simple switches, fuses, and circuit breakers are wired in series. This allows them to interrupt a circuit. With a switch in an "on" position, the circuit is closed; with a switch in the "off" position a circuit is open. A set of double-pole switches allows you to turn a circuit on or off from different places in a room. The double-pole switch is frequently used at the top and bottom of a stairway so that lights can be turned on or off from either place.

Science, Mathematics, and Technology Standards:

NSES: The Unifying Concepts in Science, including: Systems, order, and organization; and Evidence, models, and explanation. Content Standard A (inquiry); Standard B (physical science, transfer of energy); and Standard E (science and technology)

NCTM: Measurement

STL: The Nature of Technology; Abilities for a Technological World

(See **National Standards Section** for more information on each standard.)

Science Concepts: Electricity and Circuits

- Switches are used to open and close circuits.
- A switch controls the absolute flow of electricity in a circuit.
- Too many appliances, or appliances that draw large amounts of current, can cause a circuit to be overloaded, leading to overheating.
- A fuse protects a circuit from overheating by opening the circuit.
- Fuses open a circuit by burning out.
- A circuit breaker is used in place of a fuse to open a circuit.
- A circuit breaker can be reset after the load on a circuit is reduced.

See **Naive Concepts and Terminology** for more details.

Science Skills:

Students will make **observations and inferences** about circuits and their components, in particular, the battery, bulb, switch, and fuse; will **communicate** how circuits operate through the use of diagrams and descriptions; and will **manipulate materials** in the design and creation of various circuits.

See **Science Process Skills Section** for descriptions and examples.

Materials:

3″ x 5″ index card or thick cardboard of similar size	Bulbs
Paper clip	Bell wire with alligator clips
Two brass paper fasteners	Tape
Batteries	Fine-grade steel wool

(Most science supply companies or electronics stores carry commercial-type battery- and bulb-holders that may be used in these activities to make it easier for students to manipulate their materials.)

Name: _____ Date: _____

Student Inquiry Activity ⑨: Controlling the Circuit (cont.)

Content Background:

Electricity flows through a path called a circuit. The flow of electricity can be controlled by a number of different devices. Two such devices are a switch and a fuse or circuit breaker. The switch is a device with two contact points and a moveable electrical conductor that can be moved in such a way as to permit the flow of electricity or to stop it. A switch controls the entire flow of electricity. If the switch is closed, the flow of electricity is uninterrupted, and any device or devices in the circuit will operate.

As electricity flows through a circuit, the movement of the electrical charge generates heat. A greater flow of electricity through a circuit results in more heat generation. An excess amount of heat could result in the insulation surrounding the wire to start a fire, thereby causing nearby objects to burn. A fuse or circuit breaker is a device that regulates the demand of electricity flowing through a circuit. The fuse or circuit breaker allows electricity to flow as long as the demand of the appliances in the circuit does not exceed the amount of electricity allowed by the fuse or circuit breaker. If an excess demand occurs, then the fuse will melt or the circuit breaker will trip, stopping the flow of electricity. If this occurs, then the demand on the circuit must be reduced, and the fuse replaced or the circuit breaker reset.

Activity 1: The Switch

Challenge Question: How can you stop the flow of electricity in a circuit without disconnecting the battery or bulb?

Procedure:

In this activity, you will investigate methods to control the flow of electricity in a circuit. A switch is a device that stops the flow of electricity in a circuit without physically disconnecting wires.

1. To create a switch, you will use a 3" x 5" index card (or a similar-sized piece of cardboard), two brass paper fasteners, and a paper clip.
2. Make a hole in the index card for one paper fastener, approximately one-third of the way from the end of the index card.
3. Insert the paper fastener through one end of the paper clip and attach the paper clip to the index card. See diagram below.
4. Insert the second paper fastener into the index card in a location so it is touched by the other end of the paper clip.
5. Now the paper clip may be rotated to make contact with the second paper fastener. This will serve as a switch for your circuit.

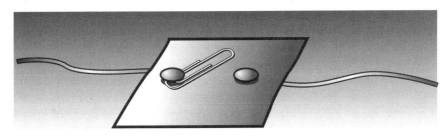

Name: _____ Date: _____

Student Inquiry Activity 9: Controlling the Circuit (cont.)

6. Now that the switch is made, you may insert it into the circuit. Attach a wire, approximately 10 cm in length, to each of the brass fasteners on the index card switch.
7. Create a circuit with one or two batteries and one bulb (similar to the previous activity, "Lighting a Bulb").
8. Select a location in your circuit to position your switch somewhere between the batteries and the bulb. Insert the switch between your battery and your bulb.

A. Close the switch in the circuit by moving the paper clip so that it touches both of the brass paper fasteners. What happens to the light bulb when the switch is closed?

_____

_____

B. Open the switch in the circuit by moving the paper clip so it does not touch one of the brass paper fasteners. What happens to the light bulb when the switch is open?

_____

_____

C. Using the symbols learned in the previous activity, draw a diagram of your circuit, including the switch.

Now label the power source, bulb, and switch.

D. List some switches that you use every day.

_____

_____

Conclusions:

E. Summarize your knowledge about switches and how they operate.

_____

_____

_____

Name: _____ Date: _____

Student Inquiry Activity 9 : Controlling the Circuit (cont.)

Summary:

A switch is used to open and close circuits. When the switch is open, the flow of electricity is interrupted, and the devices or appliances in the circuit do not operate. When the switch is closed, electricity may flow through the circuit, allowing the appliances or devices in the circuit to receive electricity and operate.

Activity 2: Fuses and Resistance

Challenge Questions: How does the size of a conductor affect its ability to conduct electricity? How does the length of a conductor affect its ability to conduct electricity?

Procedure:

A. Touch each end of a thin wire to each end of a battery at the same time. As you hold the wire to the battery, what do you notice? Explain your answer.

_____

_____

_____

B. Remove a single strand of steel wool, and then carefully tape the ends of it to a piece of paper. Attach a piece of wire to each end of a relatively fresh battery. Touch and hold the other ends of each piece of wire to the steel wool. What happens to the steel wool?

_____

_____

C. Tape another piece of steel wool to the paper. Then straighten out a paper clip and tape the paper clip to the paper as well. Create an open circuit by wrapping one end of a wire around the metal side of a light bulb, and attach the other end of the wire to one end of the battery. Next, attach a second wire to the other end of the battery. Momentarily touch the metal tip of the bulb and the end of the second wire to the ends of the steel wool and observe the bulb. Do the same with your circuit to the unfolded paper clip. Compare the brightness of the bulb in each instance.

_____

_____

D. Now tape a long piece of steel wool and a short piece of steel wool to the paper. Again touch the circuit to the steel wool at the ends of the pieces. Compare the brightness of the bulb in each instance.

_____

_____

Student Inquiry Activity 9 : Controlling the Circuit (cont.)

Conclusions:

E. Make a general statement about the brightness of the bulb and the thickness and length of the wire.

_____

_____

_____

Summary:

The flow of electricity in a circuit may be interrupted by a break in it. A switch and a fuse or circuit breaker are two ways in which a break in a circuit may occur. A switch is a device by which the interruption may be controlled. A switch is often used to turn on and off a device or appliance. A fuse or circuit breaker will also interrupt the flow of electricity, but this type of interruption is not as controlled. As electricity moves through a circuit, heat is generated. If there is too much demand on a circuit due to too many devices, excess heat will be generated. This heat could melt the insulation on wires and cause nearby substances to start a fire. A fuse or circuit breaker in a circuit will either melt or trip (deactivate) to prevent the build-up of heat.

Extensions:

1. Using a cardboard box, create a "room" in your house. Then wire a light bulb and switch in the "room" so that the light may be turned on or off.
2. Using a cardboard box, create a room with two doors. Then wire the box so it has just one light that may be turned on by one switch and turned off by the other switch, and vice-versa.

Real-World Applications:

Nearly all electrical devices include a switch to turn the device on/off. Switches come in many forms, such as the single door switch that can be used to turn an electrical device on and off from one location. A double-pole switch enables the user to turn on the electrical device from one location, and turn off the same electrical device from a different location. Switches may also be in the form of a dimmer-type switch, which can be used to control the amount of electricity flowing in a circuit.

Many electrical appliances also have fuses or circuit breakers to protect the device from overheating or receiving too much electrical energy. If the demand is so great on a circuit that the circuit begins to overheat, then the fuse will melt, or the circuit breaker will trip. In both cases, the fuse or circuit breaker will interrupt the flow of electricity.

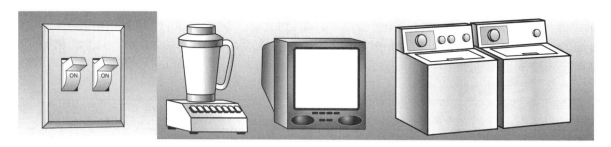

68

Name: _____ Date: _____

Student Inquiry Activity 9 : Controlling the Circuit (cont.)

Assessments:

Use the following guidelines to assess student performance. Check those statements that apply. The following represent expected responses to questions. The letters correspond to the letters on the student response sheet on the previous pages.

Activity 1: The Switch

_____ A. Student response should indicate that the light bulb lights when the switch is closed.

_____ B. Student response should indicate that the light bulb does not light when the switch is open.

_____ C. Student diagram should show the correct wiring of the circuit using the proper symbols and their labels.

_____ D. The list of switches will vary but might include: a wall switch for turning on room lamps, switches on CD players, televisions, radios, video games, or switches on lamps, microwaves, etc.

_____ E. Student response should indicate that a switch controls the flow of electrical current in a circuit. When a switch is open, current is interrupted and cannot flow. When a switch is closed, electrical current is able to flow through the circuit.

Activity 2: Fuses and Resistance

_____ A. Students should notice the wire getting warmer. The wire gets warmer because electricity is free to flow through the wire uncontrolled, and electricity flowing in a circuit will always generate a certain amount of heat.

_____ B. Student should notice the steel wool begin to smoke a little and then melt.

_____ C. Student response should indicate that the bulb shines more brightly when touched to the paper clip than to the steel wool.

_____ D. Student response should indicate that the bulb was brighter with the shorter piece of steel wool, and dimmer with the longer piece.

_____ E. Student responses should indicate an understanding that the thicker the wire, the brighter the bulb will shine, because the thick wire allows more electricity to flow through the circuit. The student's generalization should also show an understanding that the bulb will shine brighter with the shorter wire than the longer wire, because the electricity has less distance to travel within the wire; therefore, it experiences less resistance.

Name: _____ Date: _____

Student Inquiry Activity **10** : The Simple Electric Motor

Topic: The Electric Motor

This activity shows how an electromagnetic coil that is turned on and off near a permanent magnet can result in rotational motion or mechanical energy. This is the basic principle for an electric motor.

Science, Mathematics, and Technology Standards:

NSES: The Unifying Concepts in Science, including: Systems, order, and organization; and Evidence, models, and explanation. Content Standard A (inquiry); Standard B (physical science, transfer of energy); and Standard E (science and technology)

NCTM: Measurement

STL: The Nature of Technology; Technology and Society; Design; Abilities for a Technological World

(See **National Standards Section** for more information on each standard.)

Science Concepts:

• The electric motor is founded on the link between magnetism and electricity.

• A magnetic field exists in the region around a conductor, such as a wire, carrying an electric current. This is the basis for the **electromagnet**.

• Moving a conductor in a magnetic field induces a current in the conductor. Rotating the conductor in a magnetic field is the basis for a simple **electric generator**.

• An **electric generator** converts mechanical energy (rotation of the conductor) into electric energy.

• Reversing the process by supplying electric current to a conductor in a magnetic field can be used to convert electric energy into mechanical energy. This is referred to as the **motor effect**, and is the basis for the **electric motor**.

• In a generator, mechanical energy is converted to electric energy.

• In a motor, electric energy is converted to mechanical energy.

See **Naive Concepts and Terminology** for more details.

Science Skills:

Students will make **observations** about their motor as they **identify and control variables** that affect them; will **predict** how changing variables will affect their motors; will **make inferences** as to why the motor operates; will **measure** changes in their motors as **variables change**; and will **experiment** by **asking questions**, **manipulating materials**, and **analyzing the results** of their experiments.

See **Science Process Skills Section** for descriptions and examples.

Name: _____ Date: _____

Student Inquiry Activity 10 : The Simple Electric Motor (cont.)

Materials (for each group):

1 meter of #28 enameled copper wire

2 large paper clips

2 D-cell flashlight batteries

Bell wire for circuit connections

9–10 oz. plastic cup

Sandpaper

3 ring magnets

Clay

Masking tape

Content Background:

The electric motor represents the transfer of energy from one form to another. As electrical energy flows through a wire, it creates a magnetic field. In an electric motor, electricity passes through a coil of wire, producing a magnetic field nearby. The electrical coil, or armature, is surrounded by permanent magnets. Once the coil begins to spin, the two magnetic fields interact with each other. During one half of the rotation of the coil, the magnetic forces of the electric coil and the permanent magnet are attracting. During the other half of the rotation of the coil, the magnetic forces of the electric coil and the permanent magnet are repelling each other. When the force of attraction and repulsion are equal, the coil will spin. Additional gears, pulleys, or other mechanical devices may be added to the ends of the spinning armature to allow the motor to drive a piece of equipment.

Challenge Question: How can you create a simple working electric motor?

Procedure:

Making the motor:

To construct the armature or coil of the motor, begin with approximately one meter of #28 enameled copper wire. Leaving an end of about 10 centimeters of wire, begin to wrap the remaining piece of wire tightly around the circular part of a D-size battery. Wrap the wire seven times around the battery. Then, slip the loops of wire off the battery and wrap one end of the wire 3–4 times around the coil of wire to hold all seven loops together and to keep its circular shape. Then, take the other end of the wire and wrap it tightly around the coil opposite the first location in the same manner. Bend each end of the wire so it sticks straight out from each coil opposite the other. It is important that the loop is symmetrical with the ends of wire opposite each other. See the diagram below (magnified view of looped wire).

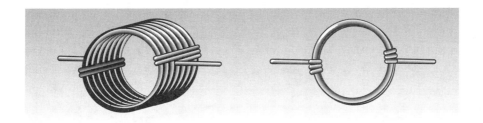

Name: _____   Date: _____

Student Inquiry Activity 10 : The Simple Electric Motor (cont.)

The enamel wire has a thin layer of enamel covering that acts as an insulator. You may trim the ends of the wire sticking straight out to a length of about 5 centimeters each. Use the sandpaper to scrape the enamel off the wire from the coil to the wire's end. This can be easily done by "gripping" the wire ends of the coil with the sandpaper and pulling the wire through your fingers while holding the wire with sandpaper. Repeating this action numerous times will remove the enamel. (Close examination of the wire will reveal that the wire is shiny, and the enamel is removed.)

You must now construct the holders for your armature or coil. Two possible ways to do this are as follows:

The Cup Holder:
Using two jumbo-size paper clips, open the paper clips into an "S" shape. Now take the smaller end of the paper clip and twist it 180 degrees, forming a small hole where the paper clip would normally bend. Do the same with the other paper clip. Turn a plastic cup upside-down and tape one paper clip on one side of the cup with the hole towards the top, and the middle of the paper clip level with the edge of the inverted cup. Now do the same with the other paper clip on the opposite side of the cup so that the two holes you formed by bending the paper clips are level. It is important that the large paper clips be fairly symmetrical with each other. (See diagram below on the left.)

The Tabletop Holder:
Using two large-size paper clips, open one to 90 degrees. Then take the larger end of the paper clip and turn it 180 degrees in its natural direction to form a small loop. Do the same with the other paper clip. Tape the two 90-degree paper clips to the table top, approximately 8 centimeters apart. The paper clips may be taped to a rigid piece of cardboard for portability. It is important that the large paper clips be fairly symmetrical with each other. (See diagram below on the right.)

Cup Holder   Tabletop Holder

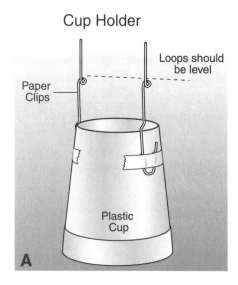

Name: _____ Date: _____

Student Inquiry Activity 10 : The Simple Electric Motor (cont.)

Lay the armature you constructed flat on the table. It is important that the armature is as balanced as possible. Be sure the two wire ends are flat on the table, are opposite each other, and point in opposite directions. Now, gently slip one end of the wire into the loop you made on one of the paper clips. Then slip the other wire into the other paper clip's loop. Gently spin the wire coil to check its balance; it should spin without any wobble. If there is wobbling, then gently bend the ends of the coil to make it balance.

Next, place a small permanent magnet on the cup or table directly below the coil. Now connect a fresh 1.5-volt battery, positive end to one paper clip, and negative end to the other. The armature may begin to spin or wobble. If it begins to spin, then CONGRATULATIONS, you have created a simple electric motor!

If the armature moves but does not spin completely around, then gently tap it to get it to spin. If the armature or coil still does not spin, recheck all of your connections to be sure the battery and wires are securely connected. The coil may try to make just a partial turn, in which case the coil is unbalanced. To balance the coil, you might have to adjust the ends of the coil where it touches the paper clips. The coil must be balanced to operate correctly. THIS PROCESS MAY BE SOMEWHAT FRUSTRATING AT FIRST, BUT CONTINUE TO WORK WITH THE MOTOR. GETTING YOUR ARMATURE TO SPIN IS A REWARDING EXPERIENCE.

Investigation:

A. Now that your motor is running, it is time to do some investigation. Predict what will happen if you add another battery in series to the current.

_____

_____

_____

B. Add the second battery and check your prediction. Was your prediction correct? Explain.

_____

_____

_____

C. Remove the second battery from the system. Predict what will happen if you add another magnet to the magnet below the armature.

_____

_____

_____

Name: _____ Date: _____

Student Inquiry Activity 10 : The Simple Electric Motor (cont.)

D. Now add the magnet, record your observations, and explain.

_____

_____

_____

Conclusions:

E. After working with your electric motor, make a generalization as to its operation and how the motor works.

_____

_____

_____

_____

Summary:

The electric coil spins due to the interaction between the electromagnet created in the armature and the permanent magnets. As current is supplied to the armature loop positioned near a permanent magnet, a distortion of the magnetic field occurs. As the electromagnetic armature interacts with the permanent magnet, the coil is repelled by the permanent magnet. As the coil rotates, the current is turned off and on due to the bounce of the armature wire. This turns the electromagnet on and off, and combined with the rotational momentum of the coil, rotation continues. The rotational momentum is just enough to maintain rotation.

Extensions:

1. Students might investigate the effect on the motor if an armature of 14 coils (twice the original number of windings) or 3–4 coils (half the original number of windings) were used.
2. Students might investigate the effect of different types of wire, such as bell wire, in the construction of the armature.
3. Students might further investigate the effects of higher voltage and/or an increased number of permanent magnets.
4. Students might investigate how the diameter of the armature affects the motor by making a larger or smaller coil.

Real-World Applications:

Electric motors are used in many ways in our daily lives. Electric motors in cars run everything from the ventilation fan to the power windows and seats, and from the windshield wipers to the alternators and starters under the hood. Small electric motors are also used to operate the turning of the CDs in your CD players and computers. Large electric motors are used in electrical generating stations to produce electricity for everyday use. Research is ongoing to develop new and more efficient motors for use in vehicles and appliances.

Name: _____ Date: _____

Student Inquiry Activity 10 : The Simple Electric Motor (cont.)

Assessments:

Use the following guidelines to assess student performance. Check those statements that apply. The following represent expected responses to questions. The letters correspond to the letters on the student response sheet on the previous pages.

_____ A & C. Student response should represent a prediction. Possible predictions might include, but not be limited to, "there will be no effect on the spin of the motor"; "the motor may spin faster, etc."

_____ B & D. Student response will vary but should include an observation of how the motor changed and a reasonable explanation as to why the change occurred.

_____ E. Student responses will vary. Response should indicate an understanding of the interaction of the magnetic fields created by the moving electrical current and the permanent magnet. Responses may also indicate a correlation between the speed of the motor and the amount of voltage supplied to the motor and a relationship between the number of permanent magnets and the motor's speed.

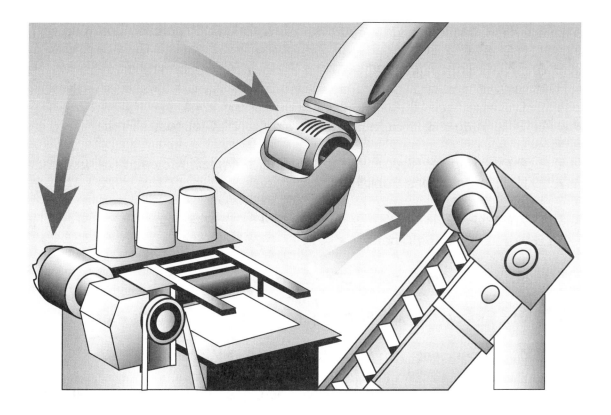

Bibliography

Children's Literature Resources:

Aczel, A.D. (2001). *The Riddle of the Compass: The Invention That Changed the World.* New York, N.Y.: Harcourt, Inc.

Berger, M. (1989). *Switch On, Switch Off.* New York, NY: HarperCollins Publishers.

Branley, F.M. (1996). *What Makes A Magnet?* New York, NY: HarperCollins Publishers.

Bryant-Mole, K. (1998). *Magnets.* Des Plaines, IL: Heinemann Interactive Library.

Chapman, P. (1976). *The Young Scientist's Book of Electricity.* Tulsa, OK: Educational Development Corp.

Cleary, B. (1983). *Dear Mr. Henshaw.* New York, NY: Bantam Doubleday Dell Publishing.

Cole, J. & Degen, B. (1997). *The Magic School Bus and the Electric Field Trip.* New York, NY: Scholastic Press.

Flaherty, M. (1999). *Science Factory: Electricity and Batteries.* Brookfield, CT: Copper Beech Books.

Gordon, M. (1996). *Electricity and Magnetism.* New York, NY: Thomson Learning.

Gunderson, P.E., (1999). *The Handy Physics Answer Book.* Farmington Hills, MI: Visible Ink Print.

Lafferty, P. (1989). *Magnets to Generators.* New York, NY: Gloucester Press.

Pinchuk, A. (2001). *Popular Mechanics for Kids: Make Amazing Toy and Game Gadgets.* New York, NY: HarperCollins Publishers.

Pinchuk, A. (2001). *Popular Mechanics for Kids: Make Cool Gadgets for Your Room.* New York, NY: HarperCollins Publishers.

Riley, P. (1999). *Magnetism.* Danbury, CT: Franklin Watts.

Tocci, S. (2001). *Experiments with Electricity.* New York, NY: Children's Press.

Tocci, S. (2001). *Experiments with Magnets.* New York, NY: Children's Press.

Whalley, M. (1994). *Experiments with Magnets and Generators.* Minneapolis, MN: Lerner Publications Co.

Bibliography (cont.)

Curriculum and Technology Resources:

Software:

Electricity CD-Rom. (2000). Bethesda. MD: Discovery Channel Science.

Magnetism CD-Rom. (2000). Bethesda. MD: Discovery Channel Science.

Macauley, D. (1998). *The New Way Things Work* CD-Rom. New York, NY: Dorling Kindersley.

Science Court: Electric Current. (1998). Watertown, MA: Tom Snyder Productions.

Science Court Explorations: Magnets. (1999). Watertown, MA: Tom Snyder Productions.

Super Solvers: Gizmos & Gadgets. (1994). Fremont, CA: The Learning Company.

ZAP: The Science of Light, Sound, and Electricity. (1998). Redmond, WA: Edmark Corporation.

Web Resources:

http://jersey.uoregon.edu/vlab/Voltage/index.html

http://www.mos.org/sln/toe/staticmenu.html

http://sln.fi.edu/franklin/activity.html

http://sln.fi.edu/franklin/scientst/electric.html

http://www.phys.virginia.edu/classes/620/electricity_activities.html

http://www.exploratorium.edu/snacks/iconelectricity.html

http://www.eskimo.com/~billb/emotor/statelec.html

Bibliography (cont.)

Curriculum Resources:

Aczel, A.D. (2001). *The Riddle of the Compass: The Invention That Changed the World.* New York, N.Y.: Harcourt, Inc.

Allen, D.S. and Ordway, R.J. (1960). *Physical Science.* Princeton, N.J.: D. Van Nostrand Company, Inc.

Allen, M., Bredt, D., Calderwood, J., Chambers, P., Deal, D., Hoover, E., Kahn, G. P., Kirkhart, J., Larimer, H., Mercier, S., Schmeling, S., Sipkovich, V., & Walsh, M. (1991). *Electrical Connections, AIMS Activities for Grades 4-9.* Fresno, CA: AIMS Education Foundation.

Marson, R. (1983). *Electricity.* Canby, OR: TOPS Learning Systems.

Marson, R. (1983). *Magnetism.* Canby, OR: TOPS Learning Systems.

Metcalfe, H.C., Williams, J.E. and Dull, C.E. (1960). *Modern Physics.* New York, N.Y.: Henry Holt and Co, Inc.

National Academy of Sciences. (2002). *Electric Circuits.* Burlington, NC: Carolina Biological Supply Company.

National Academy of Sciences. (2002). *Magnets and Motors.* Burlington, NC: Carolina Biological Supply Company.

Schafer, L.E. (2001). *Charging Ahead: An Introduction to Electromagnetism.* Washington, D.C.: National Science Teachers Association.

Schafer, L.E. (1992). *Taking Charge: An Introduction to Electricity.* Washington, D.C.: National Science Teachers Association.

Operation Physics Electricity. (circa 1989). *Electricity.* American Institute of Physics.

Operation Physics Electricity. (circa 1989). *Magnetism.* American Institute of Physics.